THE CLIMBING BOYS

ANN MURTAGH spent her first seven years in the Bronx, New York. After a short time in Dublin, her family moved to Kells, Co. Meath. She qualified as a primary teacher and later received an MA in Local History from NUI Maynooth. Local history continues to play an important role in her life and she is currently a council member of Kilkenny Archaeological Society. Ann has designed and facilitated history courses for teachers both locally and nationally. She has three sons, Daniel, Bill and Matt, and lives with her husband, Richard, and two dogs in Kilkenny City. She is also the author of *The Sound of Freedom* and *The Kidds of Summerhill*.

THE CLIMBING BOYS

ANN MURTAGH

THE O'BRIEN PRESS
DUBLIN

First published 2023 by The O'Brien Press Ltd,
12 Terenure Road East, Rathgar, Dublin 6, D06 HD27, Ireland.
Tel: +353 1 4923333; Fax: +353 1 4922777
E-mail: books@obrien.ie
Website: obrien.ie
The O'Brien Press is a member of Publishing Ireland.

ISBN: 978-1-78849-372-7

7 6 5 4 3 2 1
27 26 25 24 23

Printed in the UK by Clays Ltd, Elcograf S.p.A.

The paper in this book is produced using pulp from managed forests.

The Climbing Boys receives financial assistance from the Arts Council

Published in:

DEDICATION

In memory of my Aunt Nancy

ACKNOWLEDGEMENTS

This book was inspired by James Kelly's article 'Chimney Sweeps, Climbing Boys and Child Employment in Ireland, 1775–1875', which was sent to me by the late Michael O'Brien in November 2021. I fondly remember the lively discussions about the story that Michael and I had in the spring of 2022 and particularly feel his loss now that he isn't here to see the finished product.

Thanks to my husband, Richard, sons Bill and Matt, Rebecca Bartlett and Deirdre Murtagh for feedback on the manuscript. Matt also proved to be an insightful tour guide for the area around Pearse Street, where the story is set. I am grateful to Susan Curley-Meyer for answering some of my queries and to the Dublin City Library and Archive staff in Pearse Street for their expertise and helpfulness. I would like to thank my cousin, Colm Farrelly, for his assistance in consulting the archives, and Paul Duffy for his help with colloquialisms.

The O'Brien Press has once again been a pleasure to work with, especially my editor, Nicola Reddy. Finally, I would also like to acknowledge the Arts Council for the Agility Award I received towards funding this project.

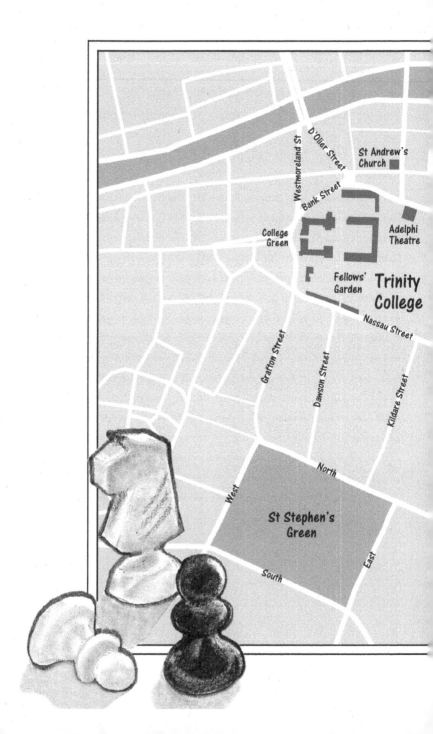

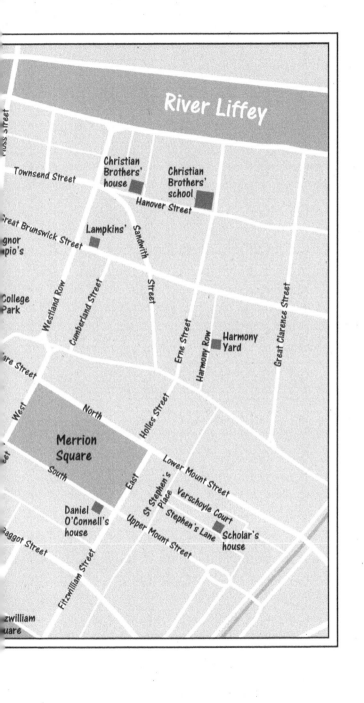

Chapter One

Christmas Eve, 1830

Before the cock crew and the neighbourhood stirred, I waded through the pitch darkness into Stephen's Lane. Guided by the map in my head, I chose where to step. Avoid the pig dung piled against the wall of Callans' next door. Don't crash into the cart full of old rags outside Nolans'. Creep past the old crate on the far side; otherwise Trusty, the hardy little terrier who lives in it, could spring out and sink her teeth into your leg. Watch this, mind that! My muscles tensed until we turned the corner into Mount Street, where the streetlamps lit the way.

Before we left home, my brothers Dexie and Cricket sat in the kitchen in the candlelight while I rubbed grease into my sore elbows and knees. This helped the cuts that smarted and the grazes that stung. None of us spoke. Ma and Da and eight other O'Dares were sound asleep in the other two rooms and wouldn't thank us for disturbing them. I was grateful for my brothers' patience; they were used to cleaning chimneys, but this was only my third week on the job. They ambled ahead of me now with their brushes and sacks. *It's only for a few months.* I often repeated those words in my head while I worked – somehow, they helped me get through the day.

The sound of hobnailed boots on the pavement behind me suddenly pulled me out of my thoughts, and I swung around.

'Hello?' I said, but the street was empty.

'Hurry up, Scholar,' Cricket called back to me. I was always called 'Scholar' at home, even though my name was Hugh. I walked faster. Panting, I caught up with my brothers.

'Heard someone behind us,' I told them.

'Probably a watchman keeping an eye out for robbers,' said Dexie.

But when I looked back, there was no lantern and no watchman in a heavy brown coat to be seen. The freezing fog dulled the streetlamps and the odd light over a front door. A black cat dashed across the footpath in front of us, disappearing through the bars of a gate.

'There you go,' said Dexie. 'Only a cat.'

'I heard boots,' I insisted.

'Did you not see the ones the cat was wearin'?' said Cricket, laughing. He was being his usual chirpy self – true to his nickname 'Cricket'. Christy was his real name. He gave me a friendly punch on the arm. 'Come on. A black cat crossed in front of us. Sign of good luck, don't forget.'

Cricket could be right. Maybe I'd be lucky enough to meet the owner of the first house we were going to work in. My brothers had met him many times, but that was before I joined them – before I became a climbing boy.

'Cheer up, Scholar,' said Dexie, as if he could read my mind. 'It's Christmas Eve, and there's a good chance you'll meet the man himself this morning. How many boys could say that?'

I smiled and agreed.

'And we've decided to give you the library, seein' you're so fond of the books,' added Cricket.

I had seen libraries in some of the houses we worked in, but not *this* library. I imagined floor-to-ceiling shelves laden with all kinds of leather-bound books. But further up Mount Street, I couldn't help looking over my shoulder again. It wasn't so much a sound as a feeling I had that somebody was following us. But there was no time to linger.

My brothers quickened their pace again until we arrived at Merrion Square. In the ghostly light of the streetlamps, the tall houses stared haughtily through their windows at the square in front of them. A watchman on the far side cleared his throat and announced the hour of four o'clock. A horse and carriage passed by. The click-clack of the hooves and the whir of the wheels faded. Dexie opened the gate of number 30, and we climbed down the steps to the servants' entrance.

On my right stood Cricket, two inches taller than me. At fourteen, he was still an apprentice chimney sweeper, learning the trade from Da, a 'master'. Dexie, at sixteen, had finished his apprenticeship and was now a journeyman sweeper, well

11

on his way to becoming a master. He was head and shoulders over me. Ma said he shot up after he turned fifteen. I couldn't wait for this to happen to me. I was fed up with being small. My brother Tim, a year younger, was now the same height as me; a few times lately, we were asked were we twins. I felt a twinge of envy as I thought of Tim, tucked up at home under the old coats and blankets.

Cricket rapped on the basement door, which opened and threw some light outside. Mrs Sullivan, the housekeeper, stood on the doorstep.

'Good morning, boys, I'll –'

Something caught her attention behind us. I felt myself being pushed aside. A tall, gangly man squeezed in between Cricket and me, his crooked nose the sign of a fighter.

'Darby Madden, Master Sweep at your service.'

'Told you I heard someone following us,' I said to my brothers. The man had one hand on his brush, the other on the shoulder of his apprentice, whom he thrust forward. The boy's hunched shoulders were covered in a torn jacket, and he kept his eyes down as he clutched his soot bag.

Dexie swung around to face the man. 'I don't care who you are, *Master Sweep*. We've been given the job here, so you can take yourself off.'

'I'll do the work cheaper,' the sweep said, ignoring Dexie and speaking to Mrs Sullivan. 'Me and the young lad here. You'll be right happy with the pair of us.'

'Will you hold your whisht!' said Mrs Sullivan. 'People are trying to sleep.'

'Hmmph,' I said, looking at his climbing boy. I wondered if he was Darby Madden's son. I was small for twelve, and this puny boy barely came up to my shoulder. I kept my voice to a whisper. 'You don't look fit to climb a lamppost, let alone a chimney flue.'

The climbing boy made a face at me but never spoke.

'Hold your tongue if ye know what's good for ye,' said Darby to me, out the side of his mouth. 'I'd wager my lad, Bert McCoy, could climb up a flue quicker than you'd look at one.'

McCoy, I thought. *So he's not Darby Madden's son.*

'He won't be climbin' anything here,' said Cricket.

'It's up to the Missus who'll get the job,' said Darby Madden. 'She looks like a practical type of woman. Wouldn't you like to save your famous employer a few bob, missus?'

'If you want to save your neck, you better step back,' said Dexie.

'Stop! Enough, all of ye,' said Mrs Sullivan. 'Stand aside, please, Mr Whatever-Your-Name-Is, and may I inform you 'twas the O'Dare brothers that were sent for to clean the chimneys?'

'But —'

'I'll not hear another word from you, young man.'

'Suit yourself,' said Darby, climbing back up to the street. Passing an empty bucket, he gave it a sharp kick, sending it

13

clattering down the stone steps with an awful din. Bert stepped sideways to avoid it and scrambled after his master. I grabbed the bucket by its ice-cold handle and set it back on the step.

'The nerve of him! He better not have woken the Master and the Missus nor the rest of the family, not to mention the neighbours.' Mrs Sullivan glanced nervously around outside as she said this. She continued in her sing-song Kerry accent. 'Two things I can promise you. That man will never darken the door of *this* house to clean chimneys. *And* I'll be telling the Master about his brazen behaviour on his very doorstep this morning.'

Chapter Two

The House in Merrion Square

Dexie cleared a space on the table for the small lit lamp, pushing aside piles of plain-covered books and papers tied with crimson tape. Then he spread the dust sheets over the floor.

'What do you think of this place, Scholar?'

'I'd never leave this room if I lived here,' I said, and Dexie laughed.

Shelves from floor to ceiling were crammed with books of all sizes – even more than I had imagined – and the air had that fusty, bookish smell I loved. I quickly counted one shelf of books – twenty-seven – and calculated roughly how many shelves were in the room. Most were law books, going on the titles, but I spotted *The History of the Decline and Fall of the Roman Empire* by Edward Gibbon; my teacher had that too.

A large wooden crucifix hung on another wall – the same as the one in the Christian Brothers' house, in the room called 'The Sacred Heart Parlour'. I took off my jacket and boots.

Jesus on the cross seemed to watch my every move, as if he felt sorry for me. In one fast motion, I drew my cap over my face to below my chin. No soot would get in my eyes, nose or mouth if I could help it.

Dexie fixed the cloth in front of the fireplace.

'I'll be next door in the drawing room,' he said before he left. I passed behind the cloth, into the darkness, and started to climb up the flue. This was the moment I hated most. I'd never tell my brothers what I often feared – that while pushing up through the flue, the chimney might turn on me and choke me, like it was something alive. Though my nose was covered, I could still smell the fusty ashes. Holding my brush above my head with one hand, I pressed my back and feet against the flue to start moving up. My sore elbows and knees smarted. Piles of soot came loose. Thankfully this flue wasn't too narrow.

I heard Dexie and Cricket working on the chimney in the next room.

'Saw that travellin' sweep last week in Camden Street,' said Dexie.

'Darby Madden? He's tall enough to remember, alright.'

'Probably doesn't half feed that young lad with him. Saw *him* stealin' a bun from one of the stalls.'

'So they've been around a few days.'

'Yeah. Bessie Reilly said they're lodgin' in Mrs McGinn's cellar.' Bessie sold fish on the streets and was one of Ma's friends. She seemed to know everything worth knowing within a five-mile radius.

There was a pause before Cricket spoke again. 'Cheek of them waltzin' into our part of town, takin' our jobs.'

'Can't let them do that,' said Dexie. 'Especially now.'

'What do you mean?'

'Found out from Ma last night there's another child on the way,' said Dexie.

'What? When?'

'April. And that could change things at home. Scholar …'

The voices became muffled as Cricket coughed, and I couldn't make out what was being said after that. Ma was going to have another baby! Of course that would change things at home – new babies always did. Peggy, the youngest, was four now. We had another little brother after her called Michael, but he died before he was six months old. That was less than a year ago. Ma took it bad. The little wooden cradle Da had made for Michael still stood in the corner of their room.

'Mrs Callan could do with it, Molly,' Da had said a few months after Michael died.

'Not yet, Bartle,' was all Ma could say, and the cradle was left there ever since.

Now another baby would be rocked in it. I thought about Ma; she had complained of feeling poorly over the last couple of weeks. Hadn't she asked Auntie Joan to come and help with the Christmas dinner? Ma, a strong woman, would never ask for help in the full of her health. I should have known the signs – she was expecting again.

Brush, scrape and loosen the soot repeated in my brain. One of my knees stung from a cut, but I tried to forget the pain and concentrate on getting the chimney as clean as I could. Tough as it was to work with my brothers, wasn't I lucky I was with them and not with strangers? Dexie had taken his time to explain how things worked. Cricket was willing to show me the best way to climb, squeeze and clean, even to do it again when he knew I was finding it hard to take everything in.

I thought about what he had shown me and made sure that I was doing it right. The boys said Mrs Sullivan always checked their work carefully. The last thing I needed was to be called back for not doing a thorough job and, worse still, to be the reason why we weren't hired to clean the chimneys again. But I couldn't help wondering what had they said about me after they talked about Ma?

I became so caught up in the work and my thoughts that I almost forgot where I was. When I eventually climbed down and came out from behind the cover, who was sitting at the big desk only Daniel O'Connell himself, dipping his pen in the inkwell. He peered at me over his little spectacles in the soft light of the gas lamp. He wore a deep-red, shiny dressing gown with a matching nightcap pulled over his brown-haired wig. I often wondered about his wig, if he wore it at home or only when he was out and about.

Here was the man who had led the campaign for Catholics to have the same rights as anyone else, the man who was the first Catholic Member of Parliament. We had paid our penny every week to help his work, and hadn't Da attended some of his huge outdoor meetings where thousands of people gathered? To think I was in a room with him on my own! Although I knew there was a chance that I'd meet Daniel O'Connell this morning, I hadn't thought about how I should be if it happened. I did the first thing that came to mind and gave a deep bow.

'Come, come, young man, no need for that!' he said.

I stood up straight and watched him finish the word he was writing and press the blotting paper over it. He had added a heap of folded newspapers to all the documents on the table. Removing the pair of spectacles from his nose, he folded his arms. 'Good morning to you!'

'Good morning, sir,' I said. I wasn't sure if I should continue working or stand and talk properly.

'Leave that a minute,' he said, as if reading my mind. 'I've met your brothers before, but you must be new. What's your name?'

'Hugh, sir,' I said.

'Hugh O'Dare?' he repeated. I could hardly believe he spoke my name. 'And what age are you?'

'Twelve, almost thirteen, sir.'

'Only two years younger than Danny, my youngest son. Hugh O'Dare ... I've heard of you from the Christian Brothers. Brother Maloney is your teacher, is he not?'

'He is, sir.'

'You've a rare talent for arithmetic, I believe.'

'Well ...' I was trying to think of what to say.

'From what I hear, you have indeed. That's a great omen for your future. You're keen to get ahead, I'm sure?'

'I am, sir.'

'And you're doing a bit of work during the holidays?'

'No, sir. I've had to leave school 'cause my father broke his arm.'

'Broke his arm? I'm sorry to hear that. But you'll be returning when he's better?'

'That's the plan, sir.'

'Delighted to hear that. Your talent's a gift from God to cherish!' He paused, his eye drawn to the sack lying near the fireplace. 'And tell me, young Hugh, did your father ever consider using one of those machines for cleaning chimneys?'

I looked at him, wondering how best to answer. I couldn't think of anything to say other than the truth. 'They're very dear, those machines, Mr O'Connell.'

Daniel O'Connell knew what I meant when I said that; we could never afford to buy one.

'The reason I asked you is that poor boy in Stoneybatter – I'm still not the better about hearing what happened to him.'

'Bob O'Leary?'

'Yes. You knew him?'

'No, sir, but my father knew his master.'

'The poor child. Shocking, shocking.'

Bob O'Leary, a nine-year-old climbing boy, died at the end of November. He was working in a house over on the far side of the city, where he climbed up one flue but became confused and chose the wrong flue to come down. All the coaldust dropped into a fire below, blazing up the chimney. The poor lad never stood a chance. I started work the following week and couldn't sleep with the nightmares I kept having about Bob dying in the fire.

Dexie came in from the other room to help me sweep up the soot.

'Good morning, Mr O'Connell.'

'Good morning, Jim.' That was my brother's proper name; he got the nickname 'Dexie' from the deck of cards and his love of card playing. 'I've just been chatting to your brother about the untimely end of that poor boy in Stoneybatter.'

'A dreadful accident, sir,' said Dexie.

'Indeed it was, but a tragedy that could have been avoided. You're the third generation of O'Dares to sweep our chimneys, and you've always done a satisfactory job. But times are changing, Jim. Next time, I will have to hire a sweep who uses a machine.'

'Oh, we're always very careful, sir,' said Dexie. I could hear the worry in his voice, knowing how losing the regular job of cleaning Daniel O'Connell's chimneys would be a blow to the business. 'We wouldn't be takin' any foolish risks on the job.'

'I know. Mrs Sullivan said the same when I discussed it with her. Still, if we're serious about stopping those dreadful accidents, we must take a stand.'

We could hear Mrs Sullivan calling one of the maids from the kitchen.

'There she is now in Sergeant Major mode – the real boss of 30 Merrion Square. Given today's Christmas Eve, she'll be charging through the rooms this morning armed with holly and ivy to decorate the place. I better let you finish.'

I knew by the tone of his voice he was trying to be funny, but I also felt that what he said about Mrs Sullivan was true. Despite being the man who changed the law in the British Parliament, this woman from Kerry was in charge of his house. Dexie, looking as if he had the weight of the world on his shoulders, continued to help me fill my sack with soot and ashes.

'Goodbye, Hugh, and good luck with the arithmetic. Goodbye, Jim.'

On my way out, Daniel O'Connell opened a drawer in his desk, took out a thrupenny coin and held it out for me. 'Buy yourself a little Christmas treat, Hugh.'

My hands were so dirty I was reluctant to take it at first.

'Don't worry. I can drop it into your hand,' he said kindly.

'Thanks, Mr O'Connell. Goodbye, sir,' I said. That money would go to Ma. Buying something for myself was out of the question, but I enjoyed thinking of what that might be like.

Chapter Three

Changes

I imagined telling the boys in my class I met Daniel O'Connell. It would be another few months, but it made me happy to think about it. I imagined how our teacher, Brother Maloney, would egg me on to share what I talked to the 'Liberator' about. He loved using that word when he spoke of Daniel O'Connell, as he rolled the rs in his Clare accent. For him, Daniel O'Connell, who 'liberated' all of us Catholics by giving us our proper rights, was the greatest man who ever lived. Most boys in my class had seen Daniel O'Connell at Mass. We were warned not to stare at him, but we couldn't help ourselves. It was hard not to when the most famous man in Ireland was sitting in the church across from you.

Although we had all seen him many times, I couldn't think of anyone who could say they spoke to him, other than one boy in my class, Rats Rattigan, and the priests and the Christian Brothers. *Today that changed*, I thought as we walked down Merrion Square. I pushed all thoughts about chimneys, brushes and scrapers aside. *I met Daniel O'Connell*. Not only had I met him, but he had heard of me.

'Come on, Scholar,' called Dexie. When I started daydreaming, I sometimes dawdled and fell too far back. I ran to catch up with them. 'Da's not going to be happy when he hears about this. Losing Daniel O'Connell's custom'll be a big loss to him.'

'Nothin' we can do about it,' said Cricket. 'Still, it's goin' be hard bringin' home the news, especially with Ma –' He started coughing.

'I heard yez talk about Ma,' I said. 'Why wasn't I told?'

'She was going to tell you this evenin',' said Dexie.

'And what was all that about changes?'

Cricket coughed again, but as soon as he stopped, he spoke. 'What with Da out of work and another mouth to feed, there's a lot of changes ahead.'

My brothers looked at each other. I knew that look. Something was being kept from me.

'But Da will be goin' back, won't he?' I asked.

'He will, but the rent's goin' up and –'

Cricket stopped to cough again, and Dexie gave him another uneasy look.

'Let Da tell him, Cricket.'

'Tell me what?' I said.

'It's not my place –'

'Please, I want to know now.'

Dexie sighed. 'You might have to stay workin'.'

'What?'

'I'm sorry to be the one who's tellin' you this —' he threw Cricket a dirty look for putting him in this awkward situation — 'but you mightn't be able to go back to school.'

'Did Da say that?'

'He did, Scholar. He was goin' to tell you this evening.'

'But I can't …' I was trying to find the right words, but my brain felt scrambled.

'Look, we know you were lookin' forward to goin' back, but things don't always turn out the way we think they will. Come on,' he said kindly but firmly, 'we've got to get to the next job.'

I managed to put one foot in front of the other to follow my brothers, but inside I was screaming. I gave up school to clean chimneys on account of Da not being able to work, but the only way I found it bearable was that I *was* going back. My nickname 'Scholar' was given to me with good reason: I loved school. School was where I learned all sorts of ways to work on numbers, like algebra and bookkeeping. It was where our teacher, Brother Maloney, set up a school library so we could borrow books.

You're keen to get ahead, I'm sure. Those words were spoken by Daniel O'Connell only a few minutes ago. How often had I daydreamed of working with a quill, calculating numbers and living in a comfortable house? I often saw myself in a room with a warm fire and a chess set on a table in the corner. I had learned how to play chess this year and loved the game, so it quickly slotted into the pictures I had in mind for the future.

And thinking of the future, I had been looking forward to learning about navigation too. Brother Maloney said he'd start it in the last term to help boys who wanted to become sailors. That made me think of Sinbad the Sailor and the stories I read about him. I used to imagine being beside him, our compass and lead line at hand as we sailed off on a voyage. Like my other dreams, the dream of learning navigation skills was now gone up in smoke. *Probably up a chimney that needs sweeping*, I thought bitterly. What was ahead of me? Navigating my way up one chimney after another. My stomach churned like a ship out in Dublin Bay tossed about in a storm.

★ ★ ★

As my mind turned over this new future, I realised that it also meant I wouldn't be able to see Izzy Everard anymore. That could only happen if I went back to school, as there was no time to meet her in the afternoons while I was working. And, of course, the real truth was I didn't want her to know that I was working as a climbing boy. Even if I were to go back to school, meeting her again would be tricky. I'd have to explain why I hadn't seen her since the end of November.

I first met Izzy in early September. One of the older Christian Brothers walked into our classroom and whispered to

Brother Maloney. After handing him a sheet of folded paper, he left again.

'Lads, I've an urgent message for Signor Sapio,' said Brother Maloney. He scanned the faces in front of him and stopped at me. 'Hugh, will you take it to him in Great Brunswick Street? It's the house beside Jones's, the coal merchants.'

'Yes, Brother.'

'Just hand it in. You don't have to come back with an answer. School's almost over, so you can go home once it's delivered.'

I took the folded sheet of paper and sprinted down the street. Arriving out of breath at Signor Sapio's door, I banged the brass knocker hard and fast. Izzy, one of his maids, opened the door. Wisps of black curly hair peeked out beneath her little cap. Her brown eyes grew larger as a little tan and white terrier dashed out behind her and onto the street. He looked playfully back at her and started running.

'Figaro!' Izzy shouted. 'Come back, you little scamp!'

Her cheeks flushed reddish pink when she shouted. I never saw that happen to a girl's face before.

'I'll get him,' I said, 'but first, give this message to Signor Sapio, please!' I pushed the piece of paper into her hand. 'It's from Brother Maloney, and he said it's urgent.'

I raced after the dog – who ran fast despite his short, butty legs – past the statue maker, the builder's yard, the grocer and the Adelphi Theatre. I had to weave in and out through people to keep after him. He was whizzing around the corner into

College Green when two boys on the street managed to catch him. They were older than me. The taller one, in a ragged jacket and trousers, held Figaro, while the younger one with two missing teeth stood in front.

'Thanks,' I said, though neither boy looked friendly.

'You want your dog back? It'll cost you,' said the missing-teeth boy.

'It's not my dog. I'm getting him for somebody else.'

'Getting him for somebody else?' repeated the missing-teeth boy. 'That's an old one.'

'Oldest one in the book,' said the boy holding Figaro. 'Bet you're after stealin' it.'

'I did not!' I shouted. I tried to push past the missing-teeth boy to grab the little dog, but the taller boy dodged me by swinging around, and they both laughed. A smartly dressed man walking out of Trinity College stopped when he spotted Figaro.

'What's going on here?'

'This fella tried to steal this little dog, mister,' said the boy with the missing teeth.

'He's lyin'! I was runnin' after him to bring him back to his owner,' I said.

The man peered at me through his spectacles and then turned again to the missing-teeth boy. 'Who's he stealing the dog from?'

'Don't know the owner's name, mister, but we knew by the

way he was after the dog that it wasn't his.'

'I know who owns him,' I said. 'It's Signor Sapio, and the dog's name is Figaro. He ran away, and I said I'd bring him back.'

'Put that dog down this instant.' The man said these words quietly but fiercely. The two boys looked at each other and decided nothing could be gained by staying. The boy holding Figaro dropped him as if his fingers were on fire and started running. The missing-teeth boy followed.

Figaro obviously knew this tall, lanky man, and judging by the way the little dog's tail went into a wagging frenzy, he must have liked him. 'He has a taste for wandering, this one,' said the man. His face softened as he patted Figaro's head. 'Hard to cure a dog of that. And your name is?'

'Hugh O'Dare.'

'Richard Webb's my name. You've done a good turn, Hugh. Signor Sapio loves this dog and would hate anything to happen to him.'

As I picked Figaro up, a man approached Mr Webb with his arm extended to shake his hand. 'Webb, my dear fellow, delighted to see you at the meeting last night.'

He shook Mr Webb's hand so fast that I thought it would come off. This was a good time for me to leave. I carried Figaro back to Sapio's and knocked on the hall door once again.

'Yes?' said a woman in a crisp white apron. Her hair, a mixture of black and grey, was scooped back into a tight bun, and there were smudges of flour on her chin.

'Here's Figaro, missus,' I said, handing her the dog. She made a face and stood back.

'Izzy!' she shouted. 'It's for you!'

I was left standing with Figaro in my arms. Izzy arrived wearing a blue cloak and took Figaro from me.

'Thanks. You've saved me from tearing down the street after him. I gave that note to Signor Sapio as soon as you left.' She opened the nearest door inside, and Figaro trotted in.

'There he is, sir,' she said, firmly closing it and moving back to the front door.

'My name is Izzy,' she said.

'And I'm Hugh,' I told her. 'Who was the woman who answered the door?'

'That's my Aunt Honorah. She's the housekeeper.'

'Not a dog lover, I'd say.'

'Indeed, she's not,' Izzy said with a smile, and two dimples appeared on her cheeks. 'That's why I'm in charge of Figaro. Can't believe you got him back so quickly.'

'It might have been a lot longer. Two boys caught him and were looking for money to give him back.'

'Oh no! Signor Sapio's been worried that might happen. What did you do?'

'A man walking out of Trinity College recognised Figaro and stopped them. They said I was running after the dog to steal him.'

'Never! What did you say?'

'I was able to name the dog and his owner, and he believed me and not them.'

'Oh, who was it? Did he give his name?'

'He said it was Richard Webb.'

'Ah, Mr Webb. A regular visitor here.' She giggled. 'Signor Sapio calls him "Ricardo". Lucky he came along. Figaro loves him. It's such a relief you got him back.' Izzy tied the ribbons of her cloak.

'Are you goin' somewhere?' I asked.

'Yes, to return these,' she said, lifting a pile of bulky books from the sideboard in the hall. They looked heavy and awkward.

'Need a hand?

She stopped and looked at me. 'Nobody ever offered to help before, but if you're going towards Sackville Street, it'd be great.'

'I'm not, but I could be.'

'Then you take these three – his Italian books – and I'll take the music books.'

That was the first time I walked to Sackville Street with this pretty, dark-haired girl in her navy-blue cloak. I found out that she was from a small town in County Kilkenny called Thomastown, and like me, she was twelve years old. Her parents died when she was very young, and her mother's cousin raised her.

'How did you come to work in Sapio's?' I asked her.

'A maid left last July, and my aunt put in a word for me.'

'What's it like?'

She paused. 'Overall, I *do* like it. My aunt can sometimes be a bit bossy but she has a kind heart behind it all.'

'And Signor Sapio?'

'He's generous, and I think he's fair.' A smile spread on her face, and she gave a little giggle.

'What's so funny?' I asked.

'I was just thinking about yesterday morning. My aunt and I were preparing the breakfast – Cook said she'd be late – and the two of us started singing "The Last Rose of Summer".'

'My mother and sisters often sing while they work, but I don't think I know that one.'

'It's our favourite,' said Izzy.

'Did you learn it at school?'

'No, I learned it from Aunt Honorah. A man who used to visit the big house in Kilkenny where she worked wrote the song, and it was sung so often all the staff knew it by heart. And now *I* know it because I heard it so often from her. Anyway, Signor Sapio came to the kitchen and clapped when we finished. Said he knew Tom Moore, the man who wrote it, and that he'd be telling him the good job we did singing it.'

As we walked along, I discovered that Izzy went to the Circulating Library in Sackville Street twice a week. I arranged to meet her the next time, and from then on, we went together. I always walked her home and felt proud to be seen with her.

What I loved about Izzy was that she *listened*. I didn't have to shout to be heard, like I did with my brothers and sisters. I didn't have to compete with a huge class of boys to get her attention like I did at school. She asked me questions and was interested in what I had to say. I did the same with her. I could talk about things with her that I couldn't with my best friend Redzer – like stories I loved to read and playing chess. Thinking about her now gave me the same feeling as warming myself at a fire after coming in from the cold.

Izzy knew I loved school because I talked to her about it more than anything else. I was the youngest in my class; Brother Maloney had promoted me ahead of time when he found out how good I was with numbers. This impressed Izzy. She hadn't spent much time in school but could read and write a little. When I got to know her better, she was even clearer that she *meant* 'a little'. She actually found reading and writing words difficult. What she loved most in school was singing; she talked about music the way I spoke about arithmetic.

Early on, she somehow got the idea that my father worked in a shop, and I didn't tell her otherwise. Nor did I tell her how many were in the family and that we were crowded into three rooms. I wanted her to see us as clean and comfortable – kind of like Redzer's family. Having a father and brothers who were chimney sweepers didn't fit into that picture.

One afternoon in October, we passed a chimney sweeper

and a climbing boy on Carlisle Bridge. The boy looked about eight years old.

'Did you see that poor little mite?' Izzy whispered.

I nodded, looking straight ahead.

'My boss belongs to a society against those boys being used to climb up chimneys.'

'Oh,' I said, trying to sound casual.

'They meet every month to discuss ways they could persuade chimney sweepers to use machines instead of climbing boys.'

'Very interestin',' I said, wondering how I could change the subject.

'We've a man coming tomorrow morning to clean the chimneys, and he'll have one of those machines. No climbing boys in Sapio's!'

Another time I spotted my older sisters, Mary and Catherine, on the far side of Westmoreland Street as I walked home with Izzy. Mary worked as a maid, and sometimes Catherine met her after work to walk home together. Luckily, they were so caught up in the chat they were having they didn't see me. That was a relief! I didn't want anyone from my family to meet Izzy. It was like leading two separate lives.

The last time I walked with her, she told me Signor Sapio cried when he heard about Bob O'Leary being burnt in a chimney. 'The poor man was beside himself with grief. His English isn't great, so some other members wrote letters to the newspapers telling the readers about what happened to Bob O'Leary and urging them not to hire climbing boys. One woman even wrote to the Prime Minister, the Duke of Wellington.'

'The Prime Minister? For what?'

'To change the law. She said boys under fourteen shouldn't be taken on to clean chimneys. Imagine she wrote to the Duke of Wellington himself to say that!'

Izzy seemed very proud of this fact. I often wondered if the Duke of Wellington ever replied. And little did she know how Bob O'Leary's death tortured me, especially the following week when I had to start working with my brothers.

What would Izzy say if she saw me today? I hadn't the courage to tell her I had to leave school because of my father's broken arm. Nor was I brave enough to admit what our family did and what I had to work at. I dreaded bumping into her on the way to or from a job, even though I knew there was a good chance she wouldn't know me if I was covered with soot. Still, there was always the chance that she might. As I thought of this, I crossed my fingers, hoping today wouldn't be the day it would happen.

Chapter Four

Saving Gwendolen

All thoughts of Izzy had to be put aside now. It grieved me to think of everything I hadn't said and should have said! I tightened my grip on the sack of soot on my back – a painful reminder that I still had a day's work ahead of me. Days and days more likely. Dexie and Cricket also carried sacks. All had to be emptied before the next job.

We sold the soot to the Lampkins at Harmony Yard, a place where chimney sweepers brought their soot and street sweepers brought the horse dung they scooped up. People came to Harmony Yard to buy the manure and soot to fertilise their gardens. As we came closer to the yard, the smell of horse manure got stronger. Beyond the heaps stood a wooden hut, now lit by a candle. Redzer Lampkin – my pal – was likely to be working today. He was still at school but worked on his days off. And sure enough, there he was inside, sitting at the table, his head of curly red hair bent over a ledger. Seeing him cheered me up. As I pressed my face against the glass of the little window to one side of the door, I was relieved to see the chess game was still out, left exactly as it was a week ago.

'Morning, lads.'

'Three sacks, Redzer,' said Dexie.

'Guess where they came from!' I said.

'I'd never guess. Tell me!' said Redzer.

'Daniel O'Connell's house.'

'What? And did you meet him?'

'I did, and he had heard about me from Brother Maloney! Can you believe that?'

'I can, of course!' said Redzer, grinning at me. 'That's some news.'

'Yes, he –' I started.

'Are you goin' to stand around all day talkin'?' said Dexie, still a little tetchy after the conversation with Daniel O'Connell. I looked at Redzer and raised my eyebrows. We could chat another time. He stayed with us while we emptied our sacks onto the nearest heap.

'Are you here for the day?' I asked.

'No. I'll leave when Mattie comes in this afternoon.'

Mattie was Redzer's older brother who had been working as a journalist with the *Dublin Newsletter* for the past six months. Redzer may have been my best friend, but I had a special regard for Mattie. Thanks to him, I learned how to play chess. One of the other journalists introduced him to the game but had since moved to London, leaving his set with Mattie. None of the Lampkins played (none of his friends were interested either), and so Mattie turned to me. From the moment he explained how to move the pieces, I loved the game. My fingers itched to finish the one on the table in the shed.

'What about your own work?' I asked Redzer.

'Lots to do back in the workshop. I've to finish a stool that has been ordered for Christmas.' The workshop belonged to his da, and Redzer worked there too. He was talented when it came to making anything with wood. 'See you tomorrow evening at the party, Scholar. Say around six o'clock?'

Lampkins' Christmas party – now *there* was something to look forward to. This was their third year to have it, so I knew what lay ahead. Redzer lived in Great Brunswick Street with his parents, brother and sister. The house had four bedrooms, a drawing room, a kitchen and a scullery. There was even enough space for a lodger – a policeman called Constable Beardwood. A huge cellar was under the house, and the yard had stables for six horses. There would be fun, games and more food than anyone could eat. This cheering-up, I could do with. Tomorrow evening, I would be out of our place faster than you could say 'mince pie'. Our home in Stephen's Lane was damp and cold. There was hardly room to scratch yourself and *never* enough food. I couldn't wait.

It was still dark on the street, but the world was waking up. Men and women muffled in cloaks, shawls and great coats hurried along the footpaths. Horses and carts clip-clopped, with an odd carriage and gig among them. Street sweepers shovelled the horse manure.

'Next stop is Herbert Place,' Dexie told us. 'We've been there once before. The servant's an old ex-army man. Very fussy about time. Best foot forward, lads.'

We put our 'best foot forward' at a brisk pace but were soon stopped by a girl running towards us, clutching a shawl around her shoulders. At first, we thought she was being chased, but nobody was after her. Holding on to the fence beside her, she tried to get her breath back to speak to us.

'Mrs Montague … Warrington Place … emergency. Can you come straightaway?'

'Is it a fire?' asked Dexie. We were often asked to put out chimney fires.

'No … But the poor woman's hysterical …'

She beckoned us to follow her. We tried to keep up with her, carrying our brushes and sacks. The girl pointed to a grand house, red-bricked with steps up to the blue front door. Mrs Montague stood on the doorstep, frantically waving at us. Straightaway we could see that she was the lady of the house and not the housekeeper.

'Here they are, Mrs Montague,' the girl called to the woman. 'Have to get back to my own work.' Off she went further down the street.

'My prayers have been answered. My maids aren't due to arrive until seven o'clock, so I had nobody to help me. Come in, come in!'

Dexie hesitated. We usually entered these grand houses at

the servants' door in the basement.

'Hurry, boys! There's no time to waste!' Mrs Montague shrieked, and we climbed the steps and followed her into the hall, stopping again at the threshold of the parlour. It was pale blue and cream with dainty cushioned chairs and no dust sheets for us to walk on. The woman beckoned us in and burst into tears. We stood looking at each other, trying to think what to say. Mrs Montague blew her nose with a big white handkerchief.

'What's the problem, missus?' asked Dexie.

'It's Gwendolen.' She pointed towards the fireplace.

'Gone up the chimney?' asked Dexie.

'She has indeed. The naughty girl. I've told her, time and again, to keep out of that filthy place, but would she listen to me? No!'

Dexie put his head into the fireplace and looked up the flue. 'Gwendolen!' he called. There was no answer. 'Gwendolen? No sign of her. What age is she, missus?'

'Six years old.'

'Six? That's young to be climbing that far. When did she go up?'

'About half an hour ago. Or was it an hour? I can't think straight. My poor darling.'

'Will you call her, missus, and see if she'll answer?'

Mrs Montague made her way over to the fireplace and shouted up. 'Gwendolen! Gwendolen! Come down this minute.'

We all waited, but Gwendolen didn't answer.

'Oh my god, she could be suffocating as we speak.'

'Don't worry, missus. We'll get her down.'

'Her mother climbed up there a couple of times, now that I think of it,' said Mrs Montague. Gwendolen must be the grandchild, we all thought. 'Her beautiful coat … It'll be destroyed.'

'Don't be worryin' about her coat, missus,' said Cricket kindly. 'Let's get her down safely. Are you ready to go up, Scholar?'

I said I was, pulled my cap over my face and started to climb. I used my shoulder and feet to push myself up. My right shoulder felt sore, as if someone had belted it, and it bruised. At least the chimney showed signs of being cleaned recently. I squeezed into the narrow section further up. Pulling my cap away from my mouth, I called, 'Gwendolen!'

I heard a little cry, which sounded very babyish for a girl of six.

'I'm comin' up to help you down.'

There was no answer to this. I stretched my arm above me to see if I could feel the little girl's foot. I felt something, alright, and I started laughing. My brothers could hear me below.

'Scholar? What's goin' on?'

I pushed myself up further and grabbed Gwendolen with both hands, using my feet and back to keep me up.

'All's good,' I said, trying my best to stop laughing. 'I've got her!'

'I'm sorry about my brother laughin',' said Dexie to Mrs Montague. 'He's new to the job and gets a bit giddy at times.'

'Be careful bringin' her down,' called Cricket up to me. 'She could be hurt.'

I prised Gwendolen out of the flue and petted her head to calm her. Once she started purring, I tucked her into my jacket and began the climb down. When we landed in the fireplace, she jumped out of my jacket and ran towards Mrs Montague.

'My precious pet,' said the woman, stroking the back of the cat's neck. 'Well done, young man.'

Gwendolen rubbed herself against the woman's skirts. Dexie and Cricket stood speechless. There were at least six chairs with cushions, and the cat jumped onto the nearest one. She yawned, stretched, curled into a ball and fell asleep. Mrs Montague didn't seem to mind that soot was all over her good furniture.

'I'll clean her later. Now, about payment,' said the woman as she walked over to a writing desk at the wall. She pulled some money out of a drawer. 'This should cover your fee. Thank you, all of you.'

Dexie wasn't going to take the money at first, but Mrs Montague insisted. It was almost twice the fee we were normally paid for cleaning a chimney. As soon as we walked down the steps of the house, we all burst out laughing.

'You were lucky you didn't have the hand scratched off you up there,' said Cricket.

'Some folk are very strange about their pets,' I said, thinking of Gwendolen on her cushion while we had a choice of three hard stools or a wooden crate to sit on at home.

Chapter Five

Darby and Bert Again

While we were saving Gwendolen, we were due at the house in Herbert Place belonging to Major Baldwin, the retired army man.

'Hurry, lads. It isn't far, but we're late. Walk as fast as you can,' said Dexie, as the bells of St Stephen's church rang out the hour. 'Cricket, remember the last job we did for the Major, when we were only a few minutes late?'

'Yeah, his servant met us with a face that would turn milk sour,' said Cricket.

'Mr Crosby?'

'That's the one,' said Cricket. 'Those old army men are sticklers for time.'

'We're much later this morning. God knows what he's goin' to be like!' said Dexie.

'Tell him about the cat,' I suggested.

Dexie laughed. 'You think he'd believe us? Leave this to me. I'll say sorry, and we'll all get to work straight away.'

We arrived at the house overlooking the canal and scrambled down the steps to the servants' entrance. Dexie took a deep breath and knocked on the door.

We waited. I motioned with my face to knock again, but Dexie shook his head. He knew from experience not to knock a second time. A key turned in the lock, and the door opened. A big, blocky, clean-shaven man stood on the doorstep. Every rib of his white hair was in place, and his shirtsleeves were neatly rolled up.

'Yes?' said Mr Crosby in a very business-like tone.

'Good morning, sir. We're here to do the chimneys. We're sorry –'

'What time is this to arrive? You're almost an hour late. When you didn't show up, I took it that you weren't coming.'

'We had to deal with an emergency, sir. That's what delayed us,' said Dexie.

'An emergency? Expect me to believe that?'

'It's the truth, sir. We could come back next week if it doesn't suit now,' said Cricket, eager to secure the job.

'It doesn't suit now' – Mr Crosby narrowed his eyes – 'nor will it suit next week. I had the good fortune to meet a chimney sweeper while delivering a message for the Master, and I have engaged *him* to carry out the work. So, I'll bid you good morning!'

He was gone, and we were left staring at a closed door.

'At least we got paid for saving that stupid cat,' said Cricket. 'What'll we do now?'

'The Christian Brothers' house,' said Dexie. 'We could get

that done.'

A roar came from inside the Major's house that made us all jump. 'Let go and get up that chimney, or I'll –'

'It's that sweeper!' I said. 'What's his name … Darby Madden.'

We all stood still and listened.

'I'm not lettin' go!' shouted another voice.

'That's his climbin' boy. Bert, isn't that what he called him? Hmm! The pair of them, still sniffing around after our work,' said Dexie.

'Is the job going to be done or not?' shouted Mr Crosby. 'Oh, for God's sake, I have no patience with the likes of this.'

'You better not cost me this job, brat!' said Darby.

'Now, now! Leave the child alone,' said Mr Crosby.

'I'll deal with the child as I see fit, thank you,' shouted Darby. This was followed by a screech, and then Mr Crosby's face appeared at the basement window. He rapped on the windowpane to tell us to wait and came running out.

'Will you come inside and tell that madman to stop?'

Dexie hesitated.

'Please?' he added.

We followed him in. Bert was holding onto a kitchen chair, and Darby was kicking his shins.

'What's goin' on?' asked Dexie, trying to get hold of Darby's arm. Darby shrugged him off.

'He wants me to go up the flue, but the fire hasn't been dampened down properly,' wailed Bert. He spoke with an

47

accent from the north of Ireland.

'Oh, boo hoo, boo hoo,' said Darby, giving Bert another sharp kick. 'Let go if you know what's good for you.'

Cricket kicked the ashes of the fire with his foot; a few glowing embers scattered among them. 'You're hardly going to ask the boy to go up in that?'

'I'll thank you not to tell me my job,' said Darby.

'Ah here, come on,' said Dexie. 'You can't blame the lad. Would you have gone up when you were a climbin' boy? Think about that.'

'And what about his indenture papers?' I chimed in.

'What about them?' asked Darby.

'Isn't there something in there about being treated fairly? My brothers' papers said that they had to be treated with "humanity and care".'

Dexie and Cricket stared at me, impressed. I don't know why I remembered those words. I came across their indenture papers recently, which had been drawn up when Da was taking them on as apprentices. The words just somehow stuck in my head. Of course, those papers were all signed with an 'x' as none of them could read or write.

Bert rubbed his sore shins. 'I could tell ye many a tale about my indenture papers,' he muttered.

'You keep your trap shut,' said Darby. He turned to Dexie. 'And I'll thank you and your family to mind your own business.'

Mr Crosby stepped forward. 'And you and your climbing boy are to leave this house immediately,' he said, like he was giving a command in the army. 'Leave, or I'll send for a policeman.'

Bert let go of the chair, and Darby grabbed him by the collar and pushed him out the door. He stepped back in and grabbed the brushes, scraper and sacks left on the kitchen floor.

'Now then,' said Mr Crosby, moving the chair back to where it had been. 'Would it be possible for you to clean the chimneys?'

'It would,' said Dexie.

I stood to his right, but my eye was drawn to a game of chess on a small table in the corner. The chessmen were beautifully carved of ivory – not like Mattie's set, which was made of wood – and given the number of pieces left on the board, I could see the game was almost finished.

Mr Crosby looked at me and cleared his throat. 'That's a game called *chess* and it isn't to be touched.'

I almost laughed out loud. The poor climbing boy mightn't know what the game was called! I didn't touch it, but I couldn't take my eyes off the chessmen as I moved towards the chimney.

'What's the matter, boy? Why are you staring at it like that?'

'Whoever's playing white better watch their back,' I said. 'Two more moves will finish the game.'

Mr Crosby looked at me as if I'd spoken a foreign language. He peered at the chessmen with his mouth open. To see him standing there, speechless, took some of the sting out of having to climb the chimney. Dexie had the widest grin I'd seen in ages, and Cricket was biting back a laugh so hard that it brought on a coughing fit.

★ ★ ★

When we were finished at Major Baldwin's, we walked into the street and stopped at the railings.

'"That game is called *chess*, I'll have you know",' said Cricket, perfectly mimicking Mr Crosby.

'I'll never forget his face when you told him how it would finish,' said Dexie. 'But that Darby Madden and his boy … We've got to do somethin' about them.'

'To stop him being a brute to the boy?' I asked, thinking about the way Darby savagely kicked him.

'Are you jokin'? It's not a charity we're runnin'.'

'But you asked Darby to stop. I just thought –'

'Look,' said Dexie, softening a little, 'I know he shouldn't have treated his boy the way he did, but we've enough on our own plates tryin' to get work for ourselves.'

Dexie sounded like Da. I could see now that he was getting more like a grown-up by the day.

'Uncle Phonsie's the man to help us,' said Cricket.

'Why not Da?' I asked.

'Phonsie has … a more direct way of dealin' with people.'

Uncle Phonsie was a hothead and a fighter – I knew the way Dexie wanted Darby dealt with.

'He'll be 'round tomorrow evening. We'll talk to him then,' said Dexie.

'Phonsie'll make sure we see the back of Mr Darby Madden and his climbin' boy for good,' said Cricket. When he noticed me looking at my feet, he added, 'What's wrong, Scholar?'

'It's just that –'

'You want us to get work, don't you?'

'Yes.'

Cricket spoke in a lower voice. 'Well, if we don't do anything, that pair will start picking up our jobs.'

'I still think it's Darby we should be after,' I said.

'There are two of them in it. We can't start makin' fish of one and fowl of the other,' said Cricket.

But I couldn't lump Bert in with Darby the way my brothers seemed to do so easily. Hadn't they done time as climbing boys themselves? And yet they were prepared to turn a blind eye to how Bert was being treated. The more I thought about it, the more uneasy I felt.

Chapter Six

Rats Rattigan and Brother Maloney

The fog had barely lifted as we walked out of Harmony Yard. The church bell rang, and Dexie said it was too late to start the Christian Brothers' chimneys.

'You'll have to go there,' said Dexie to me. 'Tell them it'll be first thing Monday mornin'. Cricket and I are headin' home.'

The two of them took off for home while I headed for Townsend Street. I ambled along Sandwith Street, my thoughts drifting towards Lampkins' Christmas party. Visions of plum pudding and gingerbread filled my head and gnawed at my empty stomach. They distracted me from noticing a boy walking towards me. He slowed down as he came closer and stared at me, trying to make out who I was beneath all the black coaldust. When I realised who *he* was, it was too late to cross the street. His voice bellowed at me.

'It's never you!'

Here was I, unlucky enough to be face to face with the

school bully, Rats Rattigan. He continued in a babyish sing-song voice.

'*A little black thing among the snow*
Crying "weep! weep!" in notes of woe.'

Of course Rats would remember the poem about climbing boys we learned in school. He blocked my way forward. 'Are you crying "weep! weep!", little Oodie, or can you say "sweep" now like a big boy?'

I couldn't pronounce some sounds when I was younger. How did Rats remember *that*? And he knew exactly how to goad me by using the name I was called when I was little.

'Shut up, Rats,' I said quietly but as fiercely as possible. 'Let me pass.'

'Oh, what's happened to our Master of Arithmetic? Calculating how far up the flue to go now, are you? And how long it'll take you to move all the dirt?'

'I'd do it faster than you,' I said.

'But the difference is, I'll never have to do mental arithmetic of *that* sort,' he said, stepping in front of me again when I tried to get past him.

Hmmph, I thought. *If you're going to work with your father in his coal business, you won't escape the dirt and dust.* I was about to say that, but a girl coming down the street behind Rats distracted me; the last person I wanted to meet.

'What a comedown for the high-and-mighty know-it-all,' Rats said, forcing a laugh.

I stood sideways, trying to hide my face. Here was Izzy, passing within a few feet of me. If I answered Rats, she'd recognise my voice. I had to stay quiet. But that very quietness irritated Rats. He pushed me, and I fell towards Izzy, managing to stop myself just in time. I held up my hand to say 'excuse me' but didn't look her in the face. She paused, and I waited for the dreaded words 'Is that you, Hugh?'

But it was Rats who spoke next, with exaggerated politeness. 'Beg your pardon, miss.' Out of the corner of my eye, I could see Izzy scowling at him. Rats brushed his hand on his jacket, mumbling, 'Good God, the dirt ...'

'Are you addressing me?' asked Izzy coldly.

'No, miss. Talking to myself,' said Rats, with that horrible false sweetness in his voice. 'Good afternoon to you.'

Izzy never answered and kept walking. Rats then spoke in a lower, menacing voice. 'The bright future everyone thought you had doesn't look too bright now, does it?'

I still could be heard by Izzy, who was only a short way down the street, so I didn't answer. I stood looking Rats straight in the eye.

'Cat got your tongue?' he said. It was clear that my silence was still bothering him. When I stepped sideways to pass him, he also stepped sideways and blocked me.

'As for school ... seems unlikely you'll ever come back. If

you ask me, you're doing what you're made for.'

I could have replied to him now – Izzy was well out of earshot – but seeing how well silence worked, I never spoke a word. I kept my head high and stared at him. When I tried to pass him this time, he didn't stop me, and we both went our separate ways.

* * *

'Good morning,' said Brother Maloney at the door of the house in Townsend Street. His clothes were pressed and spotless, making mine look ten times dirtier. 'Wait, it's you, Hugh. Didn't recognise you for a minute.'

'That's alright, Brother,' I said to my old teacher. 'Sorry, we couldn't get here this morning. Got delayed at some of the other jobs. Dexie said we'll be with you first thing on Monday mornin'.'

'Grand, grand,' said Brother Maloney, rolling his rs in that familiar Clare accent. I could sense he was looking at the coaldust and feeling uncomfortable. 'And when will we see yourself back in the classroom?'

Should I tell him the truth? I didn't feel like it. 'When Da's arm is better. He says it'll take another couple of months.'

'We'll look forward to that. Thank you for sending back that book, by the way.' He meant *Tales from Shakespeare,* the last library book I had borrowed. 'You know we were talking about you in class during the week. The lads miss you. James Rattigan was asking when his rival would be back.'

'James Rattigan?' The teachers and his parents were the only people to call Rats by his proper name.

'You look surprised,' said Brother Maloney.

'I am, to tell you the truth, Brother.'

'Why?'

'I just met him, and he didn't seem keen to see me back.'

'Really? What did he say?'

I was taken aback by the direct way the brother asked me this. I was never one to tell tales on other boys. Mean as Rats was, I found it hard to repeat what he had said.

'Oh, he thinks I'm better suited to workin' than bein' at school.' The brother waited for me to go on. 'He said it in a way that made it clear I wasn't welcome back.'

The man cleared his throat. 'He knows about your father?'

'Yes, Brother.' Everyone knew about Da being laid up at this stage.

'Then I think you're grabbing the wrong end of the stick, Hugh. I'd say he meant that you're better suited to work while your father's ill — you wouldn't be welcome back until your father's better.'

I was lost for words. Brother Maloney didn't know the Rats Rattigan the rest of us knew, and he wasn't aware of how Rats covered his tracks when he taunted us. But turning what I told him around to make it look like Rats *cared*? That surprised me.

It was almost as if the truth I told was so hard for him to hear that he had to put his own spin on it. And by the way he said it, his mind was made up.

'Anyway, we'll see you on Monday, Hugh. A happy and holy Christmas to you and your family.'

I walked down Townsend Street, my head in a whirl. What if Brother Maloney had witnessed what happened between Rats and me less than half an hour ago? Then he'd know him for the two-faced rotter he was – the teacher's pet in the school and the tormentor out on the street. The only good thing about not going back to school was that I had fewer dealings with Rats. The only pity was that I had any dealings with him at all.

Chapter Seven

Christmas Day

I t was almost twelve o'clock on Christmas Eve. Da and us older ones were among the droves of people heading to the chapel for midnight mass.

'It'll be standin' room only,' Da muttered.

We came through the door up near the altar. In the front pew sat Daniel O'Connell with his two youngest sons. Rats Rattigan and his father were kneeling at the outside of the next pew, which had a little brass plate attached to it saying that it was donated by the Rattigan family. There could have been enough room for at least three of us if they moved in, but Rats took one look at me and turned his face the other way. Luckily, we found standing space further down the church to lean against the wall. Catherine and Mary joined the women on the other side.

Mass had started already. The chapel smelled of damp coats and incense. Cricket's cough was one of many to fill the chapel, but that didn't put Father Sheridan off. He made sure he could still be heard from the pulpit. As his voice droned in Latin, my eyelids drooped, and even my numb fingers and frozen toes couldn't keep me awake. Dexie elbowed me twice when my eyes closed fully and I started to lean against him.

At one point, I was startled out of my trance when Father Sheridan thumped the pulpit and raised his voice. 'As you can see, there isn't enough room in this chapel. That is why a new one must be built, my dear people. The bishop is looking at plans and is determined to get the building started as soon as possible. We expect each family to contribute, however small. A group of men from the parish committee will go from house to house to collect the money every month.'

We were all happy that a new church was being built, but coming up with the money would be hard on our family and other families in the parish.

But all thoughts of money were put aside as the choir sang 'O Come, All Ye Faithful', giving us a Christmassy feeling.

As we left the church, we passed Daniel O'Connell, deep in conversation with Charlie Rattigan. Rats was chatting with the two O'Connell boys. My sisters Mary and Catherine hummed the tune of 'The First Noel' as we walked along the dark lane home.

'Dexie was talkin' to you,' said Da to me.

'He was,' I said glumly.

'I'm sorry, son. It grieves your mother and meself to have to keep you out of school. First one in the family to read and write, you've done us proud.'

I was shocked. Da never said anything like this before.

'I wish I could change things so you could go back, but ...' He shook his head sadly.

'It's alright, Da,' I said. He looked so forlorn, I felt he needed to hear that. Anyway, what could be done?

A light shone in the lane ahead of us like the star of Bethlehem. It was from our kitchen window. Mary had decorated it with ivy before we left for Mass. She copied – as best she could – how they did it in Taylor's, where she worked as a maid. In the meantime, Ma had lit the Christmas candle, as members of her family up in Thistle Cross in County Louth had done for generations before her, she often told us.

'And you've added holly, Ma,' I said when we arrived inside.

'Bessie's friend had some left over,' said Ma. 'She dropped in a few wee sprigs after you left. You look freezin', the lot of you. Come to the hearth and warm your hands.' She moved back to make space for us to huddle around the little fire in the grate.

'It feels cold enough for snow out there,' said Da.

'According to Bessie, there *is* snow on the way,' said Ma. 'She saw a ring around the moon last night.'

Everyone had great faith in Bessie's weather forecasts.

Ma put her arm around my shoulder. 'I'm sorry about school, Scholar.'

'It's alright, Ma,' I said. I'd have to get used to climbing now. Everyone was sorry, but that didn't change the fact that I wouldn't be going back to school.

★ ★ ★

At eleven o'clock on Christmas morning, Mary and Catherine filled the bucket with water, washed the potatoes and started singing:

I saw three ships come sailing in
On Christmas Day, on Christmas Day,
I saw three ships come sailing in
On Christmas Day in the morning.

They scraped off the potato skins to the rhythm of the music, taking turns with the verses and singing the chorus together. Ma joined in, singing in harmony. She hadn't eaten any breakfast, but now her cheeks were tinged with a rosy colour – proof that she was feeling better as the day went on. Taking one of the turnips off the table, she cut it up and peeled it. We loved to hear her sing. My sister Alice, two years younger than me, started dancing around a wicker basket that had arrived from Dundalk yesterday. Granny had sent us a goose, as she did every year.

'Careful,' called Da, as Alice nearly tripped over it. It was a matter of pride to Granny to send this from her little farm. She meant well, and we were glad to get it, but there was very little for each of us by the time it was cooked and divided up. Last year, Dexie had cracked a joke when he saw his plate that she must have sent a wren instead of a goose. Ma was *not* amused.

Auntie Joan arrived to pluck the bird, and joining in the song, she lifted it out of the basket and brought it outside. Soon after, she left to go back to Uncle Phonsie and their own family, and we all finished the tasks we were set.

There were eleven of us but we only had six plates, so there was fierce arguing about who would be in the first or second lot to eat. We all loved Granny's goose, but the plum pudding – wrapped in muslin and made in October – was the highlight for us all. Ma had it heating in a saucepan on the fire for what seemed like an eternity, filling the house with the smell of fruit and spices and steaming up the windows.

'Will you cut the puddin' up, Scholar?' asked Ma. I was asked because I'd cut it evenly and fairly. I used Da's sharp knife to cut slices. Each person had to come and take a piece and eat it with their hands.

Ma was tearful as she took hers. 'To think that little Michael was with us this time last year. Remember how he'd smile at us like we were his whole world.'

Da put his arm around her. 'Indeed I do. He was the grandest little baby.'

Nobody spoke for a minute. An image of Michael looking up at me and grinning flashed before me, and the pain of missing him came back.

'Ah, Ma, don't be sad,' said Alice. 'I thought you sang "Three Ships" this morning better than you ever did.'

Ma had to smile at this.

'Lovely puddin', Ma,' said Mary. 'As good as what they'd serve in Taylor's.'

'Best ever,' I said, and there were murmurs of agreement.

Ma tried to smile but couldn't stop the tears from filling her eyes.

'Here, Ma, you can use my hankie,' said Tim. He handed her a torn piece of faded cotton that he had pulled out of his pocket. Again, Ma tried to smile, but we all knew that Tim reminded Ma of Michael, with his mop of thick black hair.

'Ah, Tim, I'm alright now. I just need a wee minute.'

I looked at Ma. Michael was my little brother, but she was his *mother*. It was hard for me, but how much harder must it be for her? Still, I couldn't understand why she wanted another baby when she had all of us. She knew better than anyone there was rarely enough food in the house to feed us.

'Now, now, are you alright, Molly?' asked Da.

Ma said she was.

'That's good. We've nice tea and a bag of boiled sweets to look forward to later, thanks to the thruppence Mr O'Connell gave to Scholar.' He stopped and looked guiltily around. 'I'll have to admit I tried one earlier, and it was as good as Aggie Murphy's sweets at the Donnybrook Fair.'

That was where Da had met Ma twenty years ago, and all sweets were measured by Aggie Murphy's.

'You and your Aggie Murphy sweets,' said Ma, laughing.

'Don't forget Uncle Phonsie'll be coming over later to talk about the new chimney sweeper and his boy,' Da reminded us.

★ ★ ★

When it was near six o'clock and Phonsie still hadn't arrived, I told Da that I was invited to the Lampkins' party and that I'd have to leave.

'You're invited again this year?' said Ma.

I picked up a tone in her voice. 'Why wouldn't I be?'

'Oh, just that the Lampkins have become so high and mighty. I didn't think anyone from our family would be suitable guests at the Christmas party.' She said the last few words in a posh accent, and my sisters laughed.

'You can go, Scholar, but not until Phonsie is finished … goin' over the plan,' said Da.

'But –'

'Listen to your father,' said Ma. 'That party's goin' on all evening. You don't have to go so early.'

I knew I didn't *have* to, but I *wanted* to.

I decided I'd watch for Uncle Phonsie outside. That might magically make him arrive sooner. I closed the door and drifted down the lane. After the warm kitchen, my face felt raw in the freezing air. As for the weather, as usual, Bessie was right. Great globs of snow started falling from the sky. The quiet lane was no more. A riot of children laughed and screamed, hurling snowballs at their brothers, sisters and friends. It was dark out, but one or two houses had their lamps lit and shutters still open.

Still no sign of Uncle Phonsie. I was hit in the flurry of flying snowballs but made no attempt to get anyone back. My three younger brothers shouted that I was a poor sport, but I had no appetite for rough-and-tumble play right now. I was sorely tempted to keep walking out of Stephen's Lane, but I thought better. To stay warm, I jogged back to the house. Tim followed soon after, wet and cold from playing outside. He tugged at my sleeve.

'Could I go to Lampkins' party with you?' he asked as we warmed our hands on the hearth. His voice was hoarse from shouting outside.

'Sorry, Tim. Only people who are invited can go.'

'Will you ask Redzer to invite me next year?'

'I can't do that. He has to make up his own mind about who he wants to invite. You'd be the same if you were having a party.'

'No sign of Phonsie yet?' Ma asked, to change the subject. I shook my head. 'Don't worry, Scholar. He won't be long now.'

I knew she meant well, but I just wanted to go. I sat on one of the wooden boxes in the corner. Da, Dexie, Cricket, Mary and Catherine had started playing a game of cards.

'Will I deal you a hand?' asked Dexie. I told him no. I was hoping I wouldn't be sitting in the kitchen for much longer.

Out in the lane, I heard someone whistling 'We Wish You a Merry Christmas'. Uncle Phonsie put his head around the door. The cards were put away, and Ma whooshed all the younger children into our bedroom. All of us children slept in one room, and Ma and Da slept in the other. Tim hung back.

'Why can't I stay? I'm nearly as old as Scholar.'

''Cause you're not workin', son,' said Da. 'Off with you, now. Your time will come.'

Tim shot me a look of envy and slunk off to the bedroom. Of all of us, he had to be the most curious, and he hated not knowing what was going on.

'And shut that door behind you,' called Ma.

Uncle Phonsie took off his coat and sat on one of the three stools in the house.

'Looks like you're in a fierce hurry to send those lads packin'.'

'It's Scholar there,' said Da. 'He's invited to a party and is mad to go.'

'I'll be quick. This is how I see things …'

He went through the plan. We would go over tomorrow to Verschoyle Court and watch Mrs McGinn's boarding house. Darby and Bert usually came back around four o'clock. I would be the 'lookout'. Once I saw them coming, I'd signal to Uncle Phonsie, Dexie and Cricket, hiding in doorways nearby. Phonsie said it was up to me to take care of the climbing boy. The three of them wanted to give Darby a fright that would see him leave the area and not come back. I listened but said nothing.

I left to go to Redzer's. Out in the lane, my boots crunched on the snow, which was deepening by the minute. I knew what was expected of me when they said I should 'take care of the climbing boy'. I was either to threaten or clobber Bert – or both.

It was hard enough for me to be a climbing boy working with my brothers, who were kind. What must it have been like for Bert to have to do the gruelling work and suffer at the hands of a heartless bully? My family could think what they liked, but I was coming up with my own plan: to give Bert the name of a safe place to get away from Darby Madden. I would tell him to go to the Christian Brothers' house. They'd look after him.

Coming close to Verschoyle Court, I almost got caught in the crossfire of a snowball war, but I managed to dodge the missiles. Some of the younger children had built a lopsided snowman and were pressing stones for buttons onto his body. A couple of boys I recognised from school were sliding on a smooth icy patch in the far corner. A boy stood outside Mrs McGinn's cellar door. Shoulders hunched, eyes fixed on the snow – it was Bert. He didn't seem to see me, or if he did, he wasn't letting on. He looked so small and thin. Then it struck me: why not use this chance to tell him to go to the Christian Brothers? But the cellar door opened, and Darby poked his head out.

'Get inside!'

Bert looked at him but remained where he was, as still as

67

the statue of St Andrew in the church.

'Get inside if you know what's good for you!' shouted Darby louder. The sliders and snowball throwers stopped, and even the snowman builders froze at the cutting tone of Darby's voice. They all watched Bert. I expected him to scurry inside, but he held his head up and practically marched in past his master.

'Don't be so mean, mister,' shouted a boy with a snowball in his hand. Darby ignored him and banged the door closed. The boy flung the snowball after him. It slapped on the door, slid down towards the step, and all the children cheered. That was all very well, but what was being said beyond that door now? Those screams of Bert yesterday! Those vicious kicks! He must be bruised and sore today. And to think of how he took his time just now and stepped in past Darby in that proud way. That took courage.

I kicked some snow on the footpath. If only Darby hadn't arrived out. I just needed a couple of seconds to tell Bert where to run to, but I didn't even get that. If I was to help Darby Madden's climbing boy, I would have to make sure I got it right tomorrow.

Chapter Eight

Lampkins' Party

'Thought you weren't coming!' said Redzer when he saw me standing at the back door. It was after seven o'clock and the party was well underway, going by the sounds from the drawing room.

'Had to wait 'til Uncle Phonsie came.' I explained quickly what was planned.

'And you're to take care of Bert?' asked Redzer.

'Yes, but I'll be doing that my own way.' I told Redzer what I had in mind.

'Good plan,' he said. 'The Brothers'll definitely help him.'

'I've to make sure I get him on his own. My whole plan depends on that.' I lowered my voice to a whisper. 'Did you think of the clothes?'

'Of course! They're left out on the bed upstairs. Go on up. I'll wait here for you.'

Redzer knew how out of place I felt at last year's party in my own clothes, so he offered to lend me some of his to wear this year. The freezing bedroom made me change as fast as I could. I paused before I left to glance in the looking glass. It was strange to be standing there in the grey jacket; instead of Redzer's freckled face and red hair popping out of it, it had my pale face and brown hair. I wished I was a few inches taller and broader to fit into the clothes, but even if they were a bit big, they were better than my own. The smell of cloves, cinnamon and raisins put the longing for food on me. I joined Redzer downstairs. He caught me by the sleeve.

'Before we go inside, I need to tell you something.'

'Yes?'

'Izzy Everard came here yesterday.'

'What?'

'Yes. She came into the workshop looking for me, and they told her where I lived. Said you had mentioned my name a few times when you used to chat.'

'What did she say? What did she want?'

He looked around to check if anyone was within earshot. 'She said you had stopped coming to the house and sent no message or explanation, and she was worried that something had happened to you.'

'Oh God, what did you say?'

'I knew you didn't want her to find out that you were working at the chimneys.'

'So, what did you tell her?'

'I said you were very busy with school tests and the likes. I even threw in that you were so busy *I* hardly saw you.'

'Thanks … I think. Did she ask where I lived?'

'I thought that might be next, but I told her I had to go – I was doing a job for my father upstairs.'

'Thanks, Redzer.'

'To be honest, I felt bad lying to the girl like that. She was so concerned about you.' This surprised me, and I struggled to think of something to say. 'Come on, the party's going well,' Redzer continued. 'Let's go in and join them.'

I followed him into the drawing room, blinking my eyes, dazzled by the brightly lit lamps. Holly and laurel decorated the windowsills and the mantelpiece. A roaring fire in the grate added to the brightness. The room smelled of wax polish, oranges and cloves. Chairs lined the walls, and all the boys and girls stood in the middle of the room.

'Welcome to the party, Scholar!' said Mattie, Redzer's brother.

'What are we playing now?' asked Redzer.

'Pass the slipper,' said Mattie, organising everyone into a circle. A cousin called Jane Kiernan, who was visiting from the country, stood in the middle with her eyes closed.

'Are you ready?' she asked.

'Yes,' said Mattie and then promptly changed places with Redzer, as she'd recognise his voice and where he was in the circle. The slipper was passed around – there were about fifteen of us there. When Jane opened her eyes, she stared hard at all the faces. Redzer's sister Nancy kept her eyes downwards and tried to look serious.

'Nancy!' Jane shouted. Nancy held up the slipper.

'I can't keep a straight face!' she said, throwing the slipper at her cousin.

'Alright, everyone,' said Mrs Lampkin, clapping her hands. 'Come downstairs to the kitchen for some refreshments.'

We drifted down into the kitchen. The big table was covered with a white tablecloth, and what a feast! Plum pudding, mince pies, roast chestnuts, jellies, gingerbread – my eyes took it all in with relish. I wanted to taste everything but not make it too obvious. I did the same as Jane and took a slice of gingerbread. Redzer took a bite out of his piece of plum pudding.

'Did you hear that this young man was talking to the Liberator yesterday?' said Redzer to Jane.

She turned to me. 'Is that true?'

'It is.'

'What luck! What did you talk about?'

Mrs Lampkin called Redzer away, so I was left to tell Jane my tale. I tried to resist stuffing my mouth with the entire slice of gingerbread and took small bites instead.

'About arithmetic and how much I like it in school,' I said, hoping she wouldn't ask too many more questions. I didn't want to tell her I was there to clean the chimney.

'And what did he say to that?'

'He said that he'd heard I was good at it, and that a God-given talent should be looked after.' I blushed as I knew that sounded like I was boasting.

'He'd heard about you? Gosh, you must be good. Where did you meet him?'

'Merrion Square.'

'Oh, his house?'

'That's right.'

'How did you come to be there?'

Think, think, I said to myself. I took another bite of the gingerbread and swallowed.

'My brother had some business, and I came along.'

'I hope you don't mind me asking so many questions, but this is exciting news.'

'I don't mind at all,' I lied. I felt a fine film of sweat on my forehead.

'What does your brother do that brought him to the Liberator's house?'

I paused, trying to think of what I could say. Imagine if I told Jane I had gone to clean the chimney. The word 'flue' came into my mind. Again, I felt that horrible feeling in my stomach, like someone had kicked me hard there. A girl nearby had put the bowl of jellies back on the table within easy reach, and I took one and popped it into my mouth, trying to buy some time. Jane waited patiently.

'He's a flueologist,' I said when the jelly was gone.

'A what?'

73

'Come, come, have a drink of lemonade,' said Mrs Lampkin as she stood between us holding a jug. 'Grab a cup from the table, Jane, and I'll fill you up.'

Jane did as she was asked.

'Why don't I take that jug and go around with it?' I asked Mrs Lampkin. 'You've got enough to do.'

'You dear, kind boy! That's so thoughtful.'

I was wearing Redzer's jacket and trousers, but she didn't let on she noticed. She handed me the jug and never was I more willing to help. But before I moved away, she spoke. 'You're looking forward to getting back to school, I'm sure?

'I am.'

Mrs Lampkin leaned over and whispered in my ear. 'Could you try to persuade Owen to stay in school – for his own good? We have his name down for St Patrick's, but he keeps saying he doesn't want to go.'

Owen was Redzer's real name, and St Patrick's was a secondary school on Arran Quay. Like all secondary schools, you had to pay a fee to attend it.

'He doesn't like school,' I said.

'But he doesn't realise the opportunity he's been given,' said Mrs Lampkin. 'His father would have given his right arm for a chance like that when he was young, but the family couldn't afford it.'

I listened and barely nodded. *That may have been what suited Tom Lampkin, but it's not what Redzer wants*, I thought. Wasn't it as clear as the nose on her face that Redzer hated school but was a born carpenter? Mrs Lampkin wasn't giving up that easily.

'If you could just have a word, is all I'm saying ...'

She moved on, and so did I. Jane was now in conversation with Nancy, sparing me the task of having to explain what a 'flueologist' was. I moved around and filled up cups and glasses. Once the jug was back on the table, I helped myself to some Christmas pudding. If they could see me at home now ...

'Any chance of a game of chess in the morning?' said Mattie.

'Every chance,' I said. 'What time?'

'Let's say ten o'clock? I'll get over before that to light the fire.'

He moved away and Redzer grabbed my elbow. 'Saw Ma talking to you.'

'That's right.' I looked to see where his mother was now, and she was out of earshot.

'I bet she asked you to talk me into staying in school,' said Redzer.

'She did.'

'I wish she would *listen* to me for a change. Same goes for Da. I can't believe they put my name down for St Patrick's and told me *afterwards.* But they're both acting peculiar these days if you ask me. You know Da wanted me to invite Rats tonight?'

'No!' I finished the last piece of pudding.

'Yes. Even when I told him some of the things he did.'

'What did he say?'

'He tried to pass it off. Said I was taking it all too seriously.'

'That reminds me of what happened today – I met Rats in the street.'

I plucked a mince pie from a tray Nancy was carrying around and took a bite. With my mouth full, I told Redzer about meeting Rats. 'And you're not going to believe who was passing by when I met him.'

'Francis?' Francis was one of Rats's cronies.

'No, Izzy! That's what made it all the harder. I couldn't open my mouth or she'd have recognised my voice.'

'Did I hear you say the word "voice"?' asked Jane, passing by. 'Don't tell me you're a great singer *and* a mathematician?'

'I'm afraid I'm in the category of "can sing" … as in "just about can sing",' I said, laughing.

'Then you can "just about sing" with all of us now!' said Mattie. 'We're going to have a sing-song. Will you round everyone up, Redzer? Scholar, can you open the desk in the drawing room and take out the music for the carols? I'll get Nancy to sit at the piano.'

I went back upstairs and lifted the lid of the mahogany writing desk under the window. The music for the Christmas carols was on top of a bundle of papers. I happened to glance at the top sheet. It was a neatly written list of donations to the 'Governors of the School in Hanover Street'. Tom Lampkin was on the school committee, and he was in charge of keeping the records and sending them in to be printed in the newspapers. Daniel O'Connell's name was top of the list for donating five pounds. Under it was Charles Rattigan, who had also given five pounds. I couldn't believe he gave the same amount as the Liberator! How pleased the Christian Brothers must have been to get a donation like that.

I must remember to tell Redzer what Brother Maloney said about Rats today, I thought to myself. Now that I knew the Brothers had received this money from the Rattigans, it made more sense that Brother Maloney took Rats's side this morning.

I closed the desk. Boys and girls were gathering for the sing-song. There were a few faces I didn't recognise. They must be Mattie's friends. It always surprised me that none of them were interested in chess. But then again, lucky for me that they weren't!

Nancy had taken one of the oil lamps from the mantelpiece and made space for it among the holly and ivy on the piano. We gathered around her. She placed her sheet on the music-holder and started playing 'The First Noel', and we all sang.

Cleaning chimneys and missing school were stashed away and left aside for the next few hours. At one point, Izzy flashed into my mind; how she'd enjoy the singing! But I let that thought float away. The same with the plan to send Darby packing and advise Bert where to go. Time enough to face all that tomorrow.

Tonight was a time for songs, stories, jokes and games. I could eat without being warned to stop because of so many other mouths to feed. I could see clearly in a well-lit room and be warmed by a well-stocked fire. I could breathe without having to smell the dampness of the walls and sit comfortably without having to watch mice scuttle across the floor. This was *my* time, and I intended to enjoy every second.

Chapter Nine

Stephen's Day

I heard Dexie laughing in the kitchen after early Mass on Stephen's Day. Somebody else was with him. I recognised the voice – it was Dexie's best friend, Joe Melody. When I arrived downstairs, they were rummaging through a stash of old clothes from the market that Auntie Joan had been putting aside over the last couple of weeks. Each tried to outdo the other to pick the most outrageous colours to dress up as Wren Boys. Out the two of them pranced in dazzling yellows, greens and reds. Dexie wore a tattered calico dress; Joe, a red shirt and baggy green trousers. He was taller than Dexie and the red shirt barely covered his broad chest. Both boys blackened their faces with coaldust.

'I don't know how you do that,' I said.

'Do what?' said Dexie.

'Cover your face with coaldust. Are you not sick of the stuff from work?'

'We don't want people to know us,' said Dexie.

'That's all part of the fun,' said Joe, grinning.

Alice picked up a dark-red jacket and put it on. One of the

sleeves was missing.

'What about girls?' she said. 'Can girls go too? I'm a great dancer.'

'Are you joking, sis? It's Wren *Boys*,' said Dexie.

Alice made a face and started dancing anyway.

Mary, who was older than Dexie, picked up a torn skirt, sniffed it and threw it back on the pile. 'I wouldn't go with them even if girls *were* allowed.'

'Why not?' said Joe. 'Is the style not up to your standard?'

Ever since Mary had started as a maid in Taylor's, my brother and his friends teased her for becoming 'uppity'.

'I couldn't give a fig about the style. It's going after a little bird and killing it that I couldn't abide.'

'But that's what's always been done,' said Joe.

'Don't care. Couldn't stomach the thought of it,' said Mary.

'I'm with you, Mary,' I said. 'Killin' a harmless little wren –'

At these words, Alice, still dancing, covered her ears with her hands and said, 'I'm not listening!' She loved birds and animals and couldn't bear to hear about them being abused.

'Do you hear him, "harmless little bird",' said Joe. 'The problem is *you're* too soft, Mary, and *you're* too young to understand, Scholar. Bet you'll be mad to join us in a couple of years. Are you ready to go, Dexie?'

Dexie muttered gruffly that he was, and they were gone before I had a chance to tell Joe he was wrong. Hunting and killing a tiny bird would never be for me. They headed off to meet up with the rest of the lads. Once they'd hunted the wren and stuck the poor creature into a holly bush tied to a pole, the gang would sing and dance up and down the neighbourhood, hoping people could spare them a few pennies.

★ ★ ★

After nine o'clock Mass, I walked down Townsend Street and hardly noticed the snow; my head was full of the chess game and the moves I'd make. And when I opened the hut door in Harmony Yard, I was happy to see Mattie had lit the fire in the grate, taking the bitter cold out of the place.

'Mornin', Scholar. Ready to play?'

'Ready and willin',' I answered.

I sat at my side of the table and waited for Mattie to take his turn. As I had control of the centre of the board, he was in no hurry. For the next two hours, nothing existed outside that game. Having time on our hands made all the difference; we could each work out a strategy. We played until there were only a few pieces on the board, with Mattie in the stronger position.

'Time to take a break,' he said, stretching his arms. 'Fancy a mince pie from yesterday?'

'Would love one,' I said.

He unwrapped two pies from a piece of linen. 'How's your Da doing?'

'Gettin' on with it. Won't be ready to go back to work for another couple of months.'

'I'd say you're looking forward to that,' he said.

'I am.'

I was wondering about telling Mattie that I wouldn't be going back to school, but something stopped me. Talking to Mattie about family and what was ahead for me didn't feel the same as talking to Redzer.

'Can you come back later this afternoon?' asked Mattie.

'Can't, I'm afraid. Wanted at home.' I definitely wasn't going to tell him what was planned for Darby and Bert. 'Are you working here tomorrow?'

'Yes, for a few hours in the morning, but I've a reporting job in the afternoon, so Da will have to get someone else to step in.'

'Redzer?'

'Not sure. There's still a backlog of work at the workshop that has to be finished, and Da wants him there. It's getting harder all the time to get this place looked after. This place ...'

'What about it?'

'I wish Da would get somebody to work in it.'

'Why doesn't he?'

'When Uncle Mattie was alive, we managed to look after it between all of us, but now that he's gone, it's much harder to keep it going.'

Old Mattie Lampkin, Redzer and Mattie's great-uncle, had

died a few months earlier. The yard had been left to Mattie and Redzer, but their Da was in charge until they were older.

'Don't know how you manage to write for the paper and mind the yard,' I said.

'It's tricky, and what makes it harder is that Da's reluctant to take any of the men in the workshop out to come down here.'

'Why don't you ask him if you could sell it?'

'It's a good earner for the family, so Redzer and I want to hold onto it. We'd just like Da to hire someone to manage it. I suppose it's early days, and he's figuring out what to do. Mind you, it's a good place to come when it's quiet to play chess and do a bit of writing.' He patted a pamphlet on a shelf below the windowsill. Printed on the top was the heading 'Dublin Anti-Slavery Society'. 'I was hoping to write an article about the campaign against slavery.'

'What? Are there slaves in Ireland?' I asked.

'No, but there are in the West Indies and America. Of course, the West Indies is a British colony. That's what makes people angry – that it's going on in a place that Britain is in charge of. You know some of the members in the society won't touch sugar.'

'Why not?'

'Because it comes from plantations where slaves do all the work. I had such good ideas for an article! Had even arranged to call on Richard Webb.'

I hadn't heard that name since the first day I ran after Figaro.

'For what?' I asked.

'He printed that pamphlet.' Mattie pointed to the bottom of the pamphlet where it said, 'Printed by Richard D. Webb, South William Street'. 'He's involved in the society. And you know who else is a member?'

'Who?'

'Daniel O'Connell.'

'So you'd get to interview him?'

'Sadly, when I suggested writing the article to my editor, he said no.'

'Why?'

'Said I was too young to write about people protesting against slavery. He called in one of the older journalists and asked him to cover it.'

'That's not fair!' I said.

'I agree! I could have done such a good job. A member of the society even lives down the street from us – an Italian called Signor Sapio.'

Talk of Signor Sapio made me think of Izzy, and I could feel my cheeks redden. I needed to change the subject. 'Aren't you gettin' anything interestin' to report on?'

'No – unless you count charity sermons and dinners as interesting. I was at a dinner before Christmas in Morrison's Hotel, and the speaker was so dull he lulled me to sleep. I had to bribe a waiter to steal the speaker's notes afterwards so I could write my article.'

I was impressed that Mattie thought of doing such a thing, but I was curious about the food on these occasions. 'Would you be given dinner yourself at the likes of that?'

'Are you joking? I'd only be fed if I was prepared to pay for it.'

He stopped. Some Wren Boys out on the street were singing, their voices getting louder and livelier by the second. I recognised the song – it was Dexie and his pals.

'I wonder if there's a story out there,' Mattie mused. 'I can see the headline now: "Reckless Wren Boys on the Rampage".'

I laughed, but then I thought about the wren and the earlier talk at home. 'I often wondered why they kill the wren.'

'It's one of those things that's been going on so long, it's hard to work out why it ever started. I once read that it had something to do with the wren betraying St Stephen.'

'A wren? How could it do that?'

'The story goes that when Stephen was hiding from the angry crowd, the wren flapped its wings over him to show everyone where he was hiding. Of course, Stephen was caught then and put to death.'

'And do you think that's true?'

'No. I also read somewhere else that hunting the wren went on long before that – before the time of Christ. I think that's more likely the truth. But either way, isn't it a horrible thing to do to a bird?'

★ ★ ★

Later, in the fading light, I found myself on 'lookout' duty, perched on a windowsill, watching the comings and goings in Verschoyle Court. The snow on the ground was now sickly grey with slush, dirt and rubbish thrown into the street. Joe Melody peeked through a broken windowpane – my second time seeing him today.

I wondered if Joe knew why I was sitting on a windowsill in the cold. My brothers might have told him what we were about – that we had come to show Darby Madden how unwelcome he was. Uncle Phonsie lurked in the nearest doorway, and my two brothers hid in the one beyond that, Cricket trying to muffle his cough. A powerful smell of onions and tripe wafted from a nearby house. Three shawled women passed me. I stood up, stamped my feet and punched one hand into the other to warm up. But no matter what I did, the cold, damp air won; I could almost feel it spreading through my veins.

It was after four o'clock. Two little barefoot boys came out of a house with boarded-up windows. One held an old piece of sacking. Yesterday's snowman had survived the day, and the sacking was added as a scarf. They stood back, admiring their handiwork, and I couldn't help but smile. But what was I doing, sitting and watching a couple of children? I stood up, alert. Couldn't let myself get distracted. Where were Darby and Bert? Maybe they weren't coming, and we should all go home.

Someone turned the corner – a tall man with a jaunty walk. A boy came after, scurrying to keep up with him. I whistled and stepped inside the nearest hallway. My uncle and brothers emerged and came up behind the pair as they got closer to Mrs McGinn's. Uncle Phonsie forced Darby to turn around, grabbed his collar with his two hands and pushed him against the wall. Dexie and Cricket stood close by on either side.

Bert pushed between my brothers and took off. He skidded in the slushy snow but kept running. Good – now was my chance.

'Follow him, Scholar!' shouted Dexie.

I tore after Bert. For someone who looked so woebegone, he was fast. I kept him in sight in Stephen's Place but couldn't see him in Mount Street. Had he turned right or left? I caught my breath and scanned the street about me. There he was, running towards Merrion Square. I followed him there and onto Westland Row, almost colliding with a driver carrying a suitcase towards his cab.

'Steady on, boy!' the driver shouted, but I kept running. When Bert turned the corner into Great Brunswick Street, I turned the corner too.

A gang of Wren Boys, their faces blackened with soot or polish, stood outside a house ahead of me. Seeing them in the street at dusk took me by surprise. I never knew of them to be out this late. They started singing:

The wren, the wren,
The King of all birds,
On St Stephen's Day
Was caught in the furze.
And though he is little,
His family is great;
So rise up, landlady,
And give us a treat.

A window upstairs opened, and a man's head appeared. 'What time of the day is this to be coming with the wren? Get lost, the lot of you!'

'Get lost yourself, ya mean skinflint!' shouted one Wren Boy who was holding the stick with the holly bush attached to the top. He was shorter than the others, and I knew that voice. He shook the bush up at the man, who slammed the window closed. I hoped I'd get by before the gang started moving again, but I wasn't fast enough. The Wren Boy who had spoken swaggered out in front of me as if he were the Lord Mayor of Dublin.

'Penny for the wren?'

'No, Rats,' I said.

'He's no money for us, boys. What'll we do?'

The others, in their colourful shirts, one or two of them wearing dresses, came closer.

'He might have money in his pocket, and he's just not

saying,' said Francis.

He and Rats stood before me while the others closed in behind me. I felt my stomach tighten like it used to in the schoolyard. 'Told you I haven't anythin'. You're wastin' your time.'

One of the boys behind gave me a dig in the back.

'Leave him alone,' said a voice. 'If he says he hasn't money, he hasn't money.'

I turned around. It was Mattie Lampkin.

'No harm done, Mattie! We were only play-acting – "give us a penny" and all that,' said Francis.

'That's not what I heard,' said Mattie.

'Francis's right. We were only joking with him,' said Rats. 'We weren't going to do anything.'

Mattie moved to face Rats. 'Joking? Don't insult me!'

'What are you going to do? Write an account in your little newspaper column?' said Rats, and all the Wren Boys laughed.

'Hah! Don't think our readers would be interested in a gang of boys who can't dance, can barely sing, going around the city carrying a dead bird,' said Mattie.

I tried to keep from laughing.

'Careful, Mattie,' said Rats. 'Remember who you're talking to.' The smugness in his voice was unbearable.

'What's that supposed to mean?'

'My father has power where it matters and wouldn't take your remarks very kindly.'

'He may have power,' answered Mattie, 'but that doesn't give *you* the right to gang up on Scholar and blatantly lie to me as to what you were about.'

Rats grappled for words to reply, but none came. One of the older boys stepped forward. 'Come on, lads. We've had enough of this lot. Let's go to the Arcade.'

Rats hesitated but joined the rest of the Wren Boys as they continued towards College Green.

'Alright, Scholar?' asked Mattie.

'I'm fine. Thanks for steppin' in. What did Rats mean about his father havin' power?'

'The coal business is doing very well, and Charlie Rattigan sees himself as an up-and-coming man. I heard he's even got a position on the parish council. Listening to Rats, you'd think he was after being appointed Lord Lieutenant.'

I laughed. 'Did you see a climbin' boy on your travels? I'm tryin' to catch up with him.'

'Saw one walking towards the Adelphi.'

'Thanks, Mattie.'

I ran again, thanking my lucky stars that Mattie had come along when he did. Rats was bad enough on his own, but in front of a gang … I shuddered to think of what he'd have done.

Chapter Ten

Bert's Secret

A stitch in my side slowed me down, but I continued up Great Brunswick Street looking for Bert. A burly man stepped out of Del Vecchio's, the shop where they made holy statues and crosses, and put his hand up to stop me as two other men carried out a large crucifix from the workshop. It was even bigger than the one in Daniel O'Connell's house – it must have been meant for a chapel. The two men brought it to a waiting cart, where the driver hovered nervously. I couldn't resist peeking in as I passed the shop's open door. A row of statues stood in the candlelit hall. As far as I could see, they were saints; the first three were St Patricks, which made me think of Redzer and St Patrick's school. In the meantime, the man driving the cart took off with the crucifix. It must have been some important customer to be dealt with on a Sunday.

Back to finding Bert, I started running again, dodging a couple of women standing outside the Adelphi Theatre with their baskets of oranges. I caught sight of a climbing boy ahead. He turned around, spotted me, then sped around the corner into an alley. Now was my chance. Bert obviously didn't realise this was a dead end, but it didn't take long for him to figure it out. The alley ended at a brick wall. On one side was a back door into the Adelphi Theatre; on the other, a small yard and a warehouse. Bert turned around, his back to the wall, and stood as tall as possible with his two fists ready. His face was red from running, and he blew a few strands of blonde hair out of his eyes and looked fiercely at me.

'Bert! I want to –'

'You've picked the wrong person to go after,' said Bert. 'Darby Madden's the man you want, not me.' He gave me a rough push.

'Hey! Watch what –'

I was stopped by a light shining onto the alley as the theatre's back door opened.

'Oi! You two!' came a voice.

We both looked over.

'Are youse workin' for Paddy?'

We both said 'No' at the same time.

'No? Then I'll have to ask yez a favour. Can't leave the theatre, or I'll be fired. We're waitin' for the boat. I need to have it backstage. Would yez run over to the warehouse beyond and ask Paddy to bring it over?'

'The boat?' I asked.

'Robinson Crusoe's boat,' said the man, as if I were Dublin's thickest boy. 'For the panto.'

Bert and I looked at each other. Something in his look said, 'this is too good to miss'.

'We will,' I answered. It felt strange running over to the warehouse, side by side. I opened the door. A smell of cut wood and glue wafted from inside. An oil lamp was lit, and we could see Robinson Crusoe's canoe on a stand.

'Paddy?' I called.

He appeared from behind a large canvas scene showing a city.

'They're ready for the boat now.' I don't know why this made me feel important, but it did.

'Right. My back is at me, and I've nobody to help. The fella they have down as my helper never showed up. Will you carry this over for me? I'll walk beside you.'

This time Bert answered that we would. I grabbed the back end, he grabbed the front, and off we went with the canoe for the panto. It was much lighter than it looked.

'Was up all night Christmas Eve workin' on it,' said Paddy, patting the canoe. 'If it wasn't finished, it'd have been *me* navigatin' the River Liffey in a real canoe to get away from the manager. He'd kill me if it wasn't ready.'

We laughed.

'My teacher's going to teach the class about navigation after Easter,' I said. I felt like adding, 'only I won't be there'.

'Is that so?' said Paddy. 'Then school's a changed place since my day. The only navigation we ever learned was how to dodge the cane the teacher had flyin' up and down to beat us.'

We crossed the alley, and Paddy unlocked the stage door. He hung the key on a hook on the wall inside.

'Robinson Crusoe,' said Bert. 'Didn't he have navigation books? That was one of my favourite books at school.'

'You read *Robinson Crusoe*?' I said, surprised. Neither of my brothers could read or write, and most climbing boys I knew were the same. 'That book's in our library in school.'

'Oh yes,' said Bert. 'I even remember the name of the chapter: "I Make Myself a Canoe".'

I wanted to tell him about my favourite part, but we had to be careful carrying the canoe around the scenery and backstage props, so I stopped talking.

'Leave it here, lads,' said Paddy, pointing to a space near the back wall. 'I'm indebted to the pair of ye. Wait here.'

While we were waiting, a man came out. He wore black eyeliner, and his cheeks were dabbed with rouge. He pranced in front of us in his silky shirt and big black boots. Bert and I stared at him.

'Alright, boys? You giving Paddy a hand?' He had an English accent.

'Yes, we are, Mr Crusoe,' I said.

'*Mr* Crusoe?' The man laughed and bowed. 'Pleased to meet you, boys.'

Out in the theatre, a couple of violins started playing 'St Patrick's Day'. I tried to figure out how an Irish dance tune would fit in with the story of *Robinson Crusoe*.

'Hear that?' asked the actor in the silky shirt. 'The manager insists on some Irish music being used. "A Dublin audience requires some of their own music," he says. Thanks for bringing over the boat.' Then Robinson Crusoe danced out the door like he was doing an Irish jig, and we laughed.

'Did you see his face?' I said to Bert.

'That's for the stage,' said Bert. 'They have to wear that stuff so people can see them from the seats at the back.'

Again, I was surprised that he'd know this. He must have been to a theatre before.

Paddy arrived back with a jar of toffees.

'Take one each,' he said after he helped himself to one. We both took one.

'Can I've another one, please? Haven't tasted a toffee in months,' said Bert. Paddy took the lid off the jar.

'Go on. Take another one each.'

We thanked him and left through the back door. As we stepped into the alley, Bert turned to me and spoke. I couldn't make out what he said with his mouth full of toffee, and I asked him to repeat it.

'Not goin' back,' he said and swallowed the sweet.

'Where are you goin'?'

'Home. I'm headin' home. I never want to lay eyes on that demon ever again.' He started to walk away.

'Wait, Bert.'

He turned around. 'My name's not Bert.'

'What?'

'Darby put that name on me. My real name's Albertha.'

I laughed uneasily. 'Albertha? It can't be. That sounds like a girl's name.'

'That's because I *am* a girl.'

I stood with my mouth open. Could this be true? I stared at the person in front of me to make sure it wasn't some sort of joke. 'But, but I – '

'Can't talk! Have to get away.' There was a quick, nervous look behind. 'I have to get away *now*.'

The voice had a girlish tone, alright. My mind started going through all my dealings with Bert or Albertha. Were there tell-tale signs I missed? I couldn't think of one. I had a million questions to ask.

'Wait!' I called, but Bert – Albertha – was gone, speeding off around the corner into the cold, damp night. I felt tired and confused, but I started running in the same direction. I stopped outside the main gates of Trinity College, looking all around me.

'Bert, I mean Albertha!' I called loudly, not caring about the looks passers-by were giving me. But there was no answer and no sign of him – I mean her. There were several ways she could have gone, and I knew I had to give up and go home. But more than once, I stopped, still shocked at what I had just found out.

I am a girl were the four words I was trying to grasp and make sense of. Darby Madden's climbing boy – a climbing girl! Why did Darby make her pretend she was a boy? After all, there *were* climbing girls. Mind you, there weren't too many. When I thought about that, I realised I had only ever *heard* of climbing girls; I had never met one. What would Da, Uncle Phonsie and my brothers make of this when I told them?

Chapter Eleven

The Runaway
Apprentice

'He told you what?'

I repeated what Albertha had said.

'And you believed that?' asked Da.

'Albertha, if you don't mind. What a posh name,' Cricket laughed.

'Can't you see?' said Dexie. 'He told you he was a girl to make you feel sorry for him. Didn't it give him the chance to take off again?'

'Yes, but I don't think he, I mean she, was makin' it up.'

'And where did he say he was runnin' to?'

'*She* didn't say. Just said she was runnin' home. But she has a Belfast accent like Mr Doherty who lives next door to Granny.'

'Maybe Scholar's right, lads,' said Ma. 'Maybe it is a girl.'

'Don't think so, Molly,' said Phonsie. 'That Darby fella probably trained him to say that. Anyway, we've told him to clear out of the area by tomorrow mornin'.'

'That's right,' said Dexie. 'We persuaded him in true O'Dare style that this wasn't the right place for him.'

'Or for his climbin' boy,' said Cricket. 'But looks like *he's* taken matters into his own hands.'

They were convinced I'd been taken in by a pack of lies. But I knew what I heard, and I believed it: Bert was a girl, and her real name was Albertha.

* * *

Later that evening, Dexie dealt the cards and the game started. I didn't play. After a couple of rounds, Da threw in his hand.

'Scholar, I need a word,' he said, grabbing his coat. 'Will you take a turn with me 'round the square?'

There was a lovely park in Merrion Square, but only people who lived in the houses around it had keys to its gates. Everyone else walked on the road outside the park railings. Our house was so crowded; this was where we went for a quiet chat.

'Can I come, Da?' asked Tim eagerly, pushing his thick black hair out of his eyes.

'Not this time, son. I want to talk to Scholar on his own.'

What was this about? Hadn't we had 'the talk' on Christmas Eve? I glanced at Ma. Would her face tell me what was going on? But she didn't give anything away. I followed Da, squelching through the slush. He said nothing for the first few minutes, but he wasn't one for talking much anyway, so this wasn't unusual.

'Is this about that climbin' boy?' I finally asked, hoping to get him started.

'Ah no,' Da said. I knew he was uneasy by the way he was chewing his lower lip. 'I know I spoke to you the other night, but things have been happenin' since.'

'And?'

'I had a chat with a man today. There's a chance you'll be able to return to school in a few months when my arm mends.'

I looked at him to make sure he was serious. 'But I thought –'

'It'll depend on gettin' plenty of work in the next few months. That's why I'm havin' a word with you, man to man.'

I started getting worried now. This sounded serious. What was I going to hear?

'You know as well as I do that we get most of our work by word of mouth. I happened to be talkin' to Charlie Rattigan earlier. He said his coal business is goin' from strength to strength, and he'd be happy to give my name to people lookin' to have their chimneys swept.'

Charlie Rattigan? What was the catch, I wondered?

'Of course *he's* lookin' for something in return. He's hopin' I'll persuade the Lampkins to sell Harmony Yard to him.'

'For what?' I asked.

'He needs more space for his coal business. As soon as Charlie sends customers our way, I'm on for encouraging Tom

Lampkin to consider sellin' Harmony Yard.'

'But it's not Tom's – it belongs to Mattie and Redzer. And it earns good money, Da. Don't think they'd be interested in sellin'.'

'But Tom could sell it on their behalf, if he got a good price. Mattie's gone writin' for the papers – he'll never be interested in it. And I couldn't see Redzer workin' in it when he's finished school.'

'What do you want me to do? Are you askin' me to say something to Redzer?'

'No, no. Wouldn't ask you to do that. Leave the Lampkins to me. It's something else. I know yourself and young Rats don't see eye to eye, and it might harm this arrangement if you were to fall out.'

'We're not friends enough to fall out,' I said.

'You know what I mean. Don't antagonise the boy.'

'What about when he antagonises me? You don't know the half of what he goes on with.'

'And to tell you the truth, I don't want to know. I'm dependin' on you not to go fightin' the lad. If he annoys you, walk away. We need to keep in with that family.'

I didn't know what to say to this.

'Think about it this way, son: the more business the Rattigans send our way, the sooner you'll get back to school.'

What could I do only agree, even if I knew it was unfair? Everything seemed to be stacked in Rats's favour. But the more I thought about it as we walked home, the more I could see it was in my interest to be careful. And I made a pledge to myself that I would be.

★ ★ ★

That night, Bessie Reilly arrived with all the local gossip and a strong smell of fish. Ma asked my sister Mary to give her one of the stools, and Bessie plopped down on it and pulled a piece of paper out of her pocket.

'One of me neighbours found this on the ground outside the church on Christmas Eve. What does it say, Scholar?'

I took the paper and glanced through it quickly. 'Looks like a ballad about Daniel O'Connell.'

'There you go, Molly. I thought there was an air of quality about it,' said Bessie to my mother.

'Why don't you read it for us, Scholar?' said Ma. Turning to the young ones arguing over a game they were playing, she added, 'Shh! Your brother's going to read!'

'It's only one verse,' I said.

'No matter,' said Bessie. 'If it's about the Liberator, I'd love to hear it.'

I started reading:

O people of Erin, a garland entwine,
The shamrock, the laurel and roses combine,

For our hero O'Connell, whose soul is divine,
For saving old Ireland, in glory, he'll shine.

Bessie repeated the lines to herself. 'Aren't those gorgeous words? I've heard that verse sung before. I'll have to get the tune into my ear to sing it.'

She took the paper back from me, folded it delicately and put it in her pocket. Bessie loved to sing ballads, and no doubt we'd hear her sing this one in the future. 'Thanks for readin' it, Scholar.' She turned to Ma. 'That fella's goin' to go places with the way he can read and write.'

Ma's look of pride when I read for friends or neighbours always made me feel as if I was the most important person in the world.

'Did you hear Phonsie and the lads gave that Darby Madden fella his marchin' orders?' asked Ma.

'I did indeed. And did you hear the latest about his climbin' boy?' said Bessie.

'What of him?' said Ma.

'He was seen beggin' for food on College Green this evening and askin' for the road to Belfast, if you don't mind.'

Ma nodded to me as if to say, 'There, Scholar, you were right about the Belfast bit'. I could see she was thinking about telling Bessie what happened with me earlier, but she decided not to, and I knew why. Ma was convinced I had been taken in by Albertha. If Bessie was told, she'd broadcast it far and wide in the neighbourhood. It would make me look foolish and Ma was having none of that. In the meantime, Bessie had more news and was peppering to continue.

'The strange thing was, he was found at the end of Cork Street.'

'Cork Street?' said Ma. 'Who told you?' She always asked this when she had doubts about what she was being told. We all knew Bessie would never spoil a story for the sake of a lie.

'Jack Delaney – you know that neighbour of Mrs McGinn's? He was deliverin' some kindlin' to a house there and found the lad cold and half-starved. He's a kind heart, has Jack. Gave the boy a crust of bread and bundled him into his cart. Brought him back to Mrs McGinn's and told that no-good Darby Madden fella to mind his apprentice properly.'

I groaned when I heard this.

'And the end of my story is that the pair left Mrs McGinn's half an hour ago.'

'Where have they gone?' I asked.

'Don't know,' said Bessie. 'But I'm sure you'll all agree they'll not be missed.'

She went on with other news from the neighbourhood and made sure to tell us that the wind was to the north, so more snow was on the way. Tim and my younger brothers cheered when they heard this.

As soon as Bessie left, Da, Dexie and Cricket congratulated each other. Hadn't they done well? Darby Madden and his climbing boy were gone. But all I could think of was Albertha, cold and starving and trying to get on the road for home. What had caused her to go astray and end up on the road for Cork? What must it be like for her now? She went through all that cold, hunger and exhaustion only to be sent back to her tormentor. If only she had waited a minute longer, I could have advised her what to do. Mind you, the Christian Brothers wouldn't have been a wise choice given that she was a girl ... but what about the House of Mercy on Baggot Street? I'd thought of that place since.

I looked at my father and brothers now, clapping themselves on the back for a job well done. It was one thing to be glad that Darby Madden was gone – I was happy about that myself – but that Albertha was still with him? That was the last thing I wanted to hear.

Chapter Twelve

The Runaway Dog

The snow came during the night, as Bessie had predicted, and we crunched our way through it as we headed up Townsend Street at five o'clock in the morning. The Christian Brothers' house was one of our favourite jobs. They regularly swept their chimneys, which made the work easier, and the housekeeper, Mrs McKenna, always gave us breakfast after we finished. I had hoped I'd meet up with Brother Maloney today, but he was out visiting.

After we had cleaned the chimneys and left the sacks of soot outside the back door, Mrs McKenna called us in. The kitchen smelled of rashers and bread fried in dripping. We took our places at the table, easing our way into the chairs which were covered with dust sheets. As I was about to sit down, Mrs McKenna swooped in and picked up a bundle of leaflets on the windowsill behind me. At the bottom of the first one were the words 'Printed by Richard D. Webb, South William Street'.

'Sorry, love,' she said, putting them on a shelf in the dresser. 'Can't let any dust get on the leaflets about the new chapel.'

'The very things I have come to collect,' said a voice. It was

Charlie Rattigan. 'Good morning, boys.'

'Mornin',' we replied.

He took the bundle from Mrs McKenna and paused at the door. 'I've just come from the chapel house. Father Sheridan said he's looking for the chimneys to be cleaned.'

'Thanks, Mr Rattigan,' said Dexie.

Charlie took a piece of paper out of his coat pocket. 'I've a few more names of people looking to have their chimneys done. Mind you, they don't want to see you until the new year, but there's the list now.' He paused, knowing that my brothers couldn't read, then left it on the corner of the table closest to me before heading back out into the snow.

This was good news. I read out the six names and addresses on the list.

'Great,' said Dexie. 'All of those are new clients. You keep that list safe, Scholar.'

The chapel house where the priests lived was on the other end of Townsend Street, so we headed off in that direction as soon as we finished breakfast. At the corner of Moss Street, a man stepped out in front of us. A tall, thin, gangly man we thought we had seen the back of.

He gave Dexie a push on his chest. 'Not so brave now, boys, when you don't have your big uncle to mind ye?'

'Leave us alone,' said Dexie, giving him a push back.

A man dressed in black was coming up the street, and Darby saw him and stopped. When he came closer, I could see why. It was the parish priest.

'Now, now, what's going on here?' said Father Sheridan. I moved back and spotted Albertha standing against the wall of the corner house.

'Just a wee disagreement, Father,' said Darby sheepishly.

'It looked like more than that to me,' said Father Sheridan, pausing to look at each of us. 'I'll remind you all that we are still in the holy season of the Birth of Our Lord and ask you to behave accordingly.'

Albertha was staring at the priest. I wondered whether she would dash up to him and ask him to save her. I tried to get her attention to have a word with her – this was my chance to tell her about the House of Mercy on Baggot Street – but she avoided looking at me.

'Of course, Father. It isn't the season to be bickering,' said Darby.

'You're not from 'round here,' said Father Sheridan, but Darby didn't get to answer. A little dog dashed between them, chased by a chocolate-brown pointer.

'Good God,' said Father Sheridan, almost losing his balance.

I recognised the tan ears and fast little legs. 'Figaro!' I shouted.

Figaro stopped and turned around when he heard my voice. He was about to come back but looked nervously at the pointer. Albertha whistled at the pointer, bent down, picked up a stick and threw it across the road. The dog immediately left off chasing Figaro and ran for the stick.

'Smart thinking, young man,' called the priest.

I picked up Figaro.

'What did you call that dog?' asked Dexie.

'Figaro. He belongs to Signor Sapio.'

'Signor Sapio,' said Father Sheridan. 'A fine man and a great supporter of the church. Take the dog home now, good lad.'

'We're on our way down to the chapel house,' said Dexie. 'We heard from Charlie Rattigan you're looking for the chimneys to be swept, Father.'

Darby made a face at Dexie when he knew the priest wasn't looking.

'Charlie told you? That man moves very fast, indeed. Only mentioned it to him – must be less than fifteen minutes ago.'

'We could do it, Father,' said Darby. 'Wouldn't charge as much, and I guarantee you, we'd do a much better job than this lot.' His look of triumph at us when he said this was sickening.

Father Sheridan turned to Darby. His voice was cold and business-like. 'Thank you, but I prefer to give work to my parishioners. Off you go now,' he said to Dexie, 'and tell Mrs Brogan I sent you.'

'Come to the chapel house after you leave that dog back,' said Dexie to me.

I moved slowly past Albertha. The pointer sat in front of her, eager to have more fun. But Albertha was making him wait, all the while scratching the snow with the stick. Then to the dog's delight, she held the stick up and sent it flying down the street. The dog raced after it.

'Come on, Bert,' said Darby. 'We're wastin' our time here.'

Albertha looked over at me and gave the fastest glance possible to where she had been scratching the snow. Darby took off down Moss Street, and before I left with Figaro, I read the word 'HELP' scratched out in big, bold letters in the snow.

★ ★ ★

Further on, I put Figaro down. He'd follow me now that we'd left the pointer behind. Would I have the courage to bring him back? The closer I got to Great Brunswick Street, the more anxious I felt. The thought of standing on the doorstep of Signor Sapio's dressed as a climbing boy and meeting Izzy after all these months filled me with dread. This situation called for a good friend. I turned towards Redzer's workshop. When I arrived, he was out in the back yard, dividing up some wood that had been delivered.

'Urgent help required,' I said, as if it was a wanted ad in the paper. 'Dog to be returned to Signor Sapio's, but finder wishes to remain anonymous.'

Redzer laughed. 'I can finish this lot later.'

'Thanks, Redzer. I'll come with you, but I won't go up to the door.'

On our way, I told him what had happened yesterday, finding out that 'Bert' was really a girl. Redzer stopped dead on the footpath.

'Never! All the talk about climbing boy Bert, and it turns out he's a girl?' He shook his head. 'What did Dexie and Cricket say?'

'They didn't believe me. They think Bert is a boy who made up that story to make me feel sorry for him so that he could run away.'

'And your ma and da?'

'They think the same.'

'What do you think?'

'I believe her. After she told me, it seemed as clear as the nose on her face that she was a girl, but we had all missed it. But there's more.' I told him about the word 'HELP' scratched in the snow.

'That's serious. Where have they gone now?'

'That's what I need to find out. I thought you might be able to help there.'

'Me?'

'Could you ask Constable Beardwood?' This was the policeman who lodged with the Lampkins.

'I don't know. He's not too keen on being asked for information. I'll have a go, but I can't promise anything. And when we find out where they're lodging?'

'That's the first step to helpin' the girl get her freedom,' I answered.

★ ★ ★

Redzer stood on the doorstep of Signor Sapio's, Figaro beside him, wagging his tail. I hid behind a horse and carriage in front of the house next door. A warm glow shone from the drawing room in Sapio's, where the lamp was lit early. A song drifted into the street.

> *'Tis the last rose of summer,*
> *Left bloomin' alone.*
> *All her lovely companions*
> *Are faded and gone.*

It was a girl's voice, sweet yet strong. I recognised the singer *and* the song. It was Izzy. Two women walking along the footpath outside slowed down to listen. I tried to signal to Redzer to wait until it was finished before he rapped the knocker, but it was too late. He gave it three loud bangs. The singing ended mid-sentence, the women hurried off, and the door opened. Izzy's aunt appeared.

'Yes?'

Figaro jumped up on her, leaving streaks of soot on her white apron. 'Mother of God, the dog. Where on earth has he been, the filth of him? Dragged through a chimney, it looks like. Get in, ya pup, ya!'

'I believe he belongs to Signor Sapio, and it's my pleasure to

112

return him,' said Redzer grandly.

'Well, it looks like it'll be our pleasure to wash him, doesn't it?' said the housekeeper, closing the door.

Before she did, Izzy peeped out with Figaro in her arms.

'Owen! I didn't realise it was you who brought this little scamp back. How on earth did you know he belonged here?'

'It was a boy on the street ... He said, "that dog belongs to the Italian singing teacher" so I guessed it had to be Signor Sapio.'

'Well, aren't you the smart one? Don't mind Aunt Honorah. It's only a few smudges of dirt. I'll give him a quick bath, and he'll be as good as new.'

It was lovely to hear Izzy talk and fuss over Figaro. I wished I was brave enough to go up and talk to her myself.

'Have you seen Hugh since?' she asked, blushing a little.

'I have indeed,' answered Redzer.

'And did you tell him I came to your house looking –'

'Izzy!' came Aunt Honorah's voice from inside. 'Come back and finish the song!'

'Was that you singing?' asked Redzer.

'Izzy!' came the voice inside, louder now.

'Have to go,' said Izzy. 'Thanks again.'

Redzer joined me down the street. 'Did you hear that?' he asked.

'The singing?'

'Yes. What a sweet voice! And did you hear her ask about you?'

'I did.'

Redzer fell quiet.

'Wasn't it lucky her aunt called her?' I said.

'I don't know about that,' said Redzer, looking away.

'What do you mean?'

'I think you'd be better off telling the girl the truth, Scholar.'

'What?' I kicked a stone off the footpath.

'She deserves to know the truth.'

'I know I *should* tell her.'

'Then why don't you?'

'It's because I *haven't* before now that makes it so hard.'

'If I were you, I'd still talk to her.'

'Would you?'

'Of course I would. I never told you this before, but I envied you having Izzy as a friend.'

'Envied me?' I couldn't believe that Redzer, who lived in a warm, comfortable house, always had lots to eat and never had to worry about money, envied me.

'I thought you were lucky to have a friend like her,' he said.

'How do you mean?'

'Someone you could walk with and talk with – a girl who wanted to be with you and listened to you. I couldn't believe you dropped her when you started working.'

'I didn't *drop* her.'

'When you stop meeting somebody out of the blue? What would you call that?'

'You'd call it, let me think …' But I couldn't think of another word. 'I couldn't see her because I had to work.'

'Come on, you couldn't have called to the house in the evening?'

'I was exhausted; that's why I couldn't do it. I can't believe you're taking *her* side in all this.'

'I'm not. I'm being honest with you, and that's why I'm saying go and talk to the girl. The longer you leave it, the harder it'll be.'

We parted ways, and I headed towards Townsend Street. Redzer's honesty rattled me. Where would I begin to explain to Izzy why I hadn't seen her in so long? It was easy for Redzer to say 'go and talk to her', but he didn't realise the courage it would take. Nor did he understand that all my courage was used up climbing chimneys every day. As I hurried to the chapel house, I tried my best to get the tune of 'The Last Rose of Summer' out of my head, but no matter what I did, it stayed with me.

Chapter Thirteen

Help Needed

The job in the chapel house was the last one lined up for the day. Back in Stephen's Lane, Dexie told Da about meeting Darby again.

'The nerve of him. We might need to visit Darby and his climbin' boy again,' Da said angrily.

'Don't think there will be any need,' said Ma. 'I was talkin' to Bessie out in the lane, and the pair of them are lodgin' with the Doyles over in Garden Lane.'

'Where's that?' asked Cricket.

'The far side of Francis Street. She heard it from one of the hawkers over there. Mrs Doyle's not one for gettin' up early, so she wasn't too pleased to be told they've a job at seven in the morning and that she'd have to call them at six.'

Bessie had several friends among the street hawkers. Selling their wares on the streets, they could easily provide up-to-the-minute information.

'Garden Lane? Not far enough away for my likin',' said Da.

'Now, Bartle, they're out of our area. Let them be,' said Ma.

'Yes, but they were back in it this morning, weren't they? They better watch out.'

* * *

Redzer was in the workshop, knee-deep in wood shavings. His da and a couple of other workers were there, so we moved out to the yard to have a quiet word.

'Are you still mad at me?' I asked him.

'Are you joking? I had my say and I moved on, which is more than I can say for the people in my family. Ma's in a huff and Da's hardly speaking to me. They're still going on about me going to school in St Patrick's. What's your news?'

'Bessie Reilly was in with Ma this mornin', and she heard where Darby and Albertha are lodgin'.'

'That's fast. I didn't even get to ask Constable Beardwood yet. And I was thinking afterwards – why don't we go straight to the police and tell them about Darby?'

'I thought about that too, and I have a bad feelin' about doin' it. It's that sneaky way Darby has about him – he could worm his way out somehow. It would work better to get Albertha in with her story first.'

'How will we do that?'

'First we need to get Albertha away from Darby,' I said.

'Agreed.'

'Are you workin' in the mornin'?'

'I'm supposed to be, but Mattie owes me a favour. I could ask him to take over for a couple of hours.'

'Let's get up early and go to Garden Lane and wait outside Doyle's for them.'

'You're not working either?'

'Nothing lined up as of now.'

'Alright – go to Garden Lane. What then?'

'We'll follow them to whatever job they're going to and wait until Albertha has to go outside with a sack of soot.'

'What time will we meet?'

'It'll have to be six. Remember, they've a job somewhere at seven. They could be leavin' the house at half-past six, and we have to allow time to get over there.'

Redzer groaned. 'If we manage to separate her from Darby, where will we bring her?'

We were both quiet, trying to think.

'She'll have to report Darby to the police,' I said, 'but before that, she'll need to go somewhere to clean up and change into girl's clothes. I wouldn't risk bringin' her to our place after all the fuss over Darby. Wouldn't know what sort of a welcome she'd get, if any. Plus, it's millin' with childer. What about the stables in your place?'

'Too many people coming and going.'

'Wait – first, we need to get her some clothes. Could you bring some?'

'Why can't you do that? You've sisters.'

'The girls in our house don't have spare clothes.'

'What about the clothes from the market for the Wren Boys? Weren't there girls' clothes in that lot?'

'Auntie Joan took whatever was left. What about your sister, Nancy?'

'She's gone to stay with her friend for a few days. I'd ask Ma if she wasn't angry at me about school … Wait a minute, there might be some old clothes of Nancy's I could rummage through. What'll I get?'

I was a bit vague about what girls wore under their dresses. 'Oh, the usual things girls wear,' I said, hoping that would cover everything.

'Right,' said Redzer uneasily.

'And where will she clean up and change?'

Redzer cleared his throat. 'I know of a good place and someone who'd help us.'

'Who?' I asked.

'Izzy. That carriage lane is very quiet, and you told me you often used to go into the back garden to play with Figaro. Weren't there sheds blocking the view from the kitchen window?'

'There were, but –'.

'And it'd be convenient to the police station in Bank Street.'

'That's true, but I'd have to tell her everythin',' I said. We were back to the old argument again. 'I don't know if she'd even talk to me.'

'I bet she would, Scholar. I think she'd really want to help Albertha, and I think telling her would be in your own interests too.'

'But not tellin' her about the chimney sweepin'... All the times she went on about it, and I said nothin'. It'd be awful admittin' it to her now. Don't know how I'd face her.'

'So you're never going to talk to her again?'

'I didn't say that.'

'And you know of someone else who could help us?'

'I'm thinkin'! I'm thinkin'!'

I imagined Izzy's face if I told her the truth. She could easily walk away for good. But Redzer was right – if I wanted to talk to her again, I needed to make a start. The longer I left it, the harder it would be.

'Look, you're being handed a reason to meet her again,' said Redzer.

I knew he was right. I'd been thinking a lot about what he had said to me last time. This was a good chance, and I'd be a fool to let it go. And there was no denying that Izzy would be the ideal person to help us.

'Alright, I'll ask her. It's Monday, so she'll be goin' home from Sackville Street this afternoon, and I'll go over that way and meet her.'

'I think you're doing the right thing.'

'We'll know soon enough.'

'If she agrees to help, I'll see you in the morning at six.'

'And if she doesn't agree?'

'Come by our house this evening, and we'll come up with another plan. Oh, but wait, Scholar – what about tomorrow night? Where will Albertha stay afterwards?'

'When I was chasin' her yesterday, I was going to tell her to go to the Christian Brothers for help – that's when I thought she was a boy. Then I thought the House of Mercy on Baggot Street would be the best place for a girl to get help. They could look after her until she goes home.'

'Fair enough. And if she doesn't want to go there, there's the hut in Harmony Yard. It's got a fireplace in it that'd keep her warm. We could get some straw and make up a bed.'

'Good idea.'

'It's quiet these days, and I'm usually there. I could set it up.'

'Thanks, Redzer. If I don't see you until the mornin', don't forget Nancy's clothes.'

★ ★ ★

I peeped into the Circulating Library. No sign of Izzy yet, but something else caught my eye. Tables and chairs were set up inside the window, and a chess game was being played. I pressed my face against the pane.

One player had his back to me. The player facing me – a pale, grey-haired man – kept rubbing his chin and staring at the board. The game was at a crucial point. If only I was playing in his place! Just as I imagined myself taking the next move, the man himself glanced at me. Lowering his eyes to concentrate on the game, he rubbed his chin again, but when he looked up and saw that I was still watching him, he stood and moved closer to the window. With a quick flutter of his hand, he told me to move away.

The other player turned around, and I recognised his face. It was Richard Webb, the man who helped me the first time I caught Figaro and whose name I had seen on the printed leaflets. He stared at me, going through his own memory. In the meantime, the old man called one of the shop assistants over and pointed to me. The assistant appeared in the doorway. He was new since I had last been in the Circulating Library with Izzy.

'Move away from the window, boy,' he said, as if I was a bad smell from the Liffey. 'You're upsetting Mr Pim's chess game.'

'I'm standin' on a public pavement,' I answered. 'I've a right to be here the same as anyone else.'

The assistant was about to answer, but somebody behind him spoke.

'Technically, the young man is correct, Luke.' Richard Webb stood in the doorway.

'Yes, sir,' said the shop assistant meekly.

'I recognise you, young fellow. Weren't you running after Figaro one day? Can't quite remember your name.'

'I was. The name's Hugh O'Dare, sir.'

'That's it. I remember saying it to Signor Sapio afterwards, and he didn't seem to know you?'

How would I reply to that – where would I even begin? Luckily, I was saved by somebody coming up behind me.

'Good afternoon to you, Richard!'

'Good afternoon to you, too,' said Mr Webb. He pushed his spectacles, which were slipping down his nose, back into place. I turned around. Daniel O'Connell stood smiling in a dark-green woollen coat with a turned-up fur collar. His tall hat had a band of shiny green ribbon around it.

'And 'tis yourself, young O'Dare. What are you up to this afternoon?'

'I was lookin' in the window at the game of chess, sir.'

'Game of chess?' repeated Daniel O'Connell.

'I'm playing Pim,' explained Mr Webb. 'He took exception to the young lad staring through the window at him. Said it was affecting his game.'

'I was only workin' out moves the man could make. Didn't mean to upset anyone, sir,' I said.

Somebody passed me walking towards the shop. That 'somebody' turned around, and I found myself face-to-face with Izzy Everard. The blood drained from her face in shock and returned with a vengeance as her two cheeks blushed bright red.

'Hello, Izzy,' said Mr Webb, standing to one side to let her in. Of course, as a regular visitor to Signor Sapio's, he knew Izzy.

'Afternoon, Mr Webb,' she replied.

'Hello ...' I started to say, but Izzy had opened the shop door and entered. I froze as if she had cast a spell over my body, turning it into lead.

'You know this boy?' Richard Webb asked Daniel O'Connell.

'I do indeed. And I know that he has a tremendous talent for numbers. I *didn't* know he also played chess,' said Daniel O'Connell.

'Does he, indeed?' asked Mr Webb, staring at me through his spectacles. I was still so rattled at seeing Izzy that I couldn't think of what to say. The Liberator stopping to talk to people on the street always attracted attention; sure enough, others were stopping now, curious to know what was happening. If I was my normal self, I'd have felt honoured and proud, but these feelings were impossible with Izzy only a few feet away. Daniel O'Connell took out his watch and checked the time.

'Must keep going. Give Pim my regards, Richard. I'll see you both at the next meeting.' Then he turned to me. 'Hope your father's health is improving?'

'It is, thanks, sir.'

He marched off, holding his umbrella over his shoulder like a gun. Mr Pim tapped the window for Richard Webb to return to the game. I stood on the pavement, going over what I could say to Izzy when she came out. Instead of sharpening my thinking, the cold air seemed to freeze it. Would I be able to find the right words at all, or should I forget the whole idea? I paced up and down and glanced through the window to see if she was still inside or had left through another door I didn't know about. But there she was at the counter. The assistant was tying up a bundle of books and handing them to her. I didn't linger so as not to upset the chess game again. Moving to one side of the door, I waited for her to come out onto the street. She saw me but didn't stop as she made her way home. I dashed after her.

'Afternoon,' I managed to say with what breath I had left.

Izzy turned her face sideways, blushed, said a very curt 'Afternoon' and kept up the fast pace.

'Sorry I haven't been around lately,' I said, trying to keep up with her.

'You've obviously moved up in the world.'

She thought this after seeing me talking to Daniel O'Connell and Richard Webb. If only she knew! She swerved to the left and disappeared into the Medical Hall before I could reply. I thought it better not to follow her and once more stood waiting on the frozen pavement. This time she came out but never spoke and kept walking. The smell from the Dublin Coffee House drifted towards us in the street. I ran ahead of Izzy and stood in front of her.

'I need to talk to you, Izzy – please.'

'Yes?' She stopped and looked at me, but there was no warmth.

'Things changed at home, and because of that, they changed for me. That's why I couldn't meet you.'

'Yes, I heard from your friend Owen that you had school tests to get ready for.'

'He made that up.'

'What are you talking about?'

'He knew I didn't want you to know the truth.'

'About what?'

'About what I'm doin' now. I had to leave school to work with my brothers.'

'Why didn't *you* let me know that?'

'I couldn't. To tell you the truth, I felt ashamed.'

'Ashamed of what?'

'Of the kind of work I'm doin'.'

'How could your work make you feel ashamed? God, you're not in a band of thieves?'

'No, of course not. It's ...'

'For God's sake, what is it? It can't be that bad.'

I took a deep breath, swallowed, and came out with it. 'I'm a climbin' boy. I clean chimneys, and my Da and brothers are all chimney sweepers.'

She looked at me to make sure I was being serious. When she saw that I was, she spoke again. 'Oh, for heaven's sake, why didn't you tell me? Why did you let me believe that your father worked in a shop?'

'I thought you'd think more of me that way.'

'And to think of how honest I was with you – about finding reading and writing hard. That took courage to admit to you.'

'I know, and I'm really sorry, Izzy.'

She stopped, looked at my face and then down at the ground. 'You don't realise how worried I was. I was afraid you were seriously ill. I couldn't face Christmas without finding out how you were. When I think of it, heading down to Lampkins' to enquire about you.'

'I thought it was very kind of you.'

'Kind? I'd call it foolish. Your friend Owen is in on the lies too, telling me that nonsense about studying for tests.'

I didn't say anything to this.

'And when I think of going on about Signor Sapio and that society he belongs to. You never said a word!' She banged one fist on the books she was carrying.

'I thought you'd think ill of me and my family because we can't afford those cleanin' machines.'

'You, you, you!' she shouted at me. We were crossing Carlisle Bridge. Even on this cold day, the river stank.

'Shhh!' I said. Passers-by were turning around to look at us.

'I don't care who's listening. You didn't think, for one minute, how it might be for *me*.'

'I did think!' I shouted back. 'I was tryin' to keep your good opinion.'

'Then you should have told me the truth!' she screamed, walking faster again, making me half-run to keep up with her.

'I wanted to see you. I really did. I even came with Owen today. It was me who found Figaro.'

'Hmm! And you didn't even have the courage to speak to me. You had to get your friend to do it.'

'Well, I was hardly going to show up on Signor Sapio's doorstep covered in coaldust and ask you to invite me in for afternoon tea.'

In the old days, Izzy would have laughed heartily at this, but her lips stayed firmly in a straight line. Suddenly she stopped and turned to me. 'What made you come and tell me all of this now?'

'I need your help.'

'So you're here only because I'm of some use to you?'

'No! I was trying to pluck up the courage to talk to you again, and something happened that made me do it quicker.'

Izzy was curious now but trying not to show it. The air was filled with the shrill voices of seagulls flying over us. *Tell her, tell her!* they seemed to be shrieking. But Izzy spoke again. 'Why me?'

'Because I trust you.'

'Trust! I've got news for you. I don't trust *you.*'

'Izzy, please, will you just hear me out?'

'Why should I?'

'Because I'm tryin' to save a girl's life.'

She paused, staring at me fiercely. She was about to reply, but I could see she couldn't think of what to say.

'Owen and me – we're tryin' to save this girl. We need help, and we thought you'd be the best person to go to.' Her face was softening. 'I *know* you're the best person to help us.'

'Start talking. Mind you, I'm not promising anything.'

I told her about Darby and Albertha – from Christmas Eve in Merrion Square to this morning. She asked the odd question.

'Please help us. Let me prove you *can* trust me,' I said.

Izzy didn't reply to this. We walked along Westmoreland Street, neither of us talking, but I glanced sideways and could see she was thinking about all I had told her. Then she stopped.

'Right, let me go through the plan. You're going to bring Albertha to Signor Sapio's so she can clean up and get changed before you bring her to that constable that Owen knows.'

'That's right, and after that, we plan on bringing her to the House of Mercy in Baggot Street. We thought the women there would help her.'

'That's a good idea.'

'And Redzer said that if she doesn't want to go to them, she could stay in the hut in Harmony Yard.'

'Hmmm … I think the House of Mercy'd be better.'

'We'll leave that up to her,' I said.

'Alright. I'll be on the lookout all morning. Bring her to the dairy.'

'What about your aunt?' I asked.

'Don't worry, I'll handle her.'

She asked me what size Albertha was, and I did my best to tell her. I told her about Redzer's sister and the clothes.

'I'll leave some clothes in the wooden box under the window in the woodshed,' she said. 'Owen's sister is a good bit older; her clothes would probably drown the girl.'

'Thanks, Izzy. And one more thing.'

'Yes?'

'I know Owen wouldn't mind if you called him "Redzer", and you can call me "Scholar". That's what I go by with my friends and family.'

Izzy smiled, and I felt so happy to see the two dimples on her cheeks like old times.

I walked back to Stephen's Lane with a lighter step. Redzer was right about telling the truth to Izzy, and I was only sorry I hadn't done it much sooner.

Chapter Fourteen

The Rescue

Fred Callan, our neighbour, closed his door with a bang on his way out to work. Time for me to get up. I scrambled through the straw on the floor and woke Tim up as I moved. His head of black hair appeared above the blankets.

'Scholar?'

'What?'

'What are you doin'?'

'Gettin' up.'

'I thought there were no jobs on this mornin'.'

'There aren't. I'm meetin' Redzer.'

'Redzer? At this hour? What are the pair of you up to?'

Tim would think nothing of following us to find out what was happening. Luckily, I was at the door when he asked me this.

'Can't stop. Have to go!'

I stumbled into the lane, grumpy and half asleep. The snow was gone, but the crisp, frosty morning shocked me awake. Redzer was waiting for me, a bundle of clothes for Albertha tucked under his arm.

'Let's go,' I said. 'Quick! Tim's awake. Wouldn't put it past him to follow us.'

We shivered as we hurried off, our breaths steaming in the frosty air, our footsteps the only sound disturbing the early morning stillness. We passed two girls sitting on the steps of the House of Mercy on Baggot Street. All going well, Albertha would be going through the door later today.

Redzer looked behind him. 'No sign of Tim. Here's some bread I grabbed on the way out.'

He produced two slices of bread and we ate as we walked.

'So, you met Izzy yesterday?' asked Redzer.

'I did.'

'And she agreed to help?'

'She did, though you couldn't say she was happy to see me at first.'

I told him all about Izzy, what we said to each other and how the conversation ended. Redzer said he was happy I had cleared the air and that Izzy was going to help us.

We walked on in silence. At Stephen's Green, a watchman peeped out when he heard us before settling back into his little hut.

'Your da was over yesterday,' said Redzer.

'Oh?'

'I overheard him talking to my father in the kitchen.'

I wondered if it was about the sale of Harmony Yard. After all, Charlie Rattigan had started sending work our way.

'He was talking to Da about Harmony Yard, how it would be a good time to sell,' said Redzer, as if he had read my mind.

'And what did your da say?' I tried to look surprised.

'Da reminded him that it was left to Mattie and me.'

'And that was the end of it?'

'No, your da was quick enough to point out that neither Mattie nor myself had much interest in the yard. Then he whispered something, and I barely caught what was said.'

'I'm all ears.'

'He said Charlie Rattigan would like to buy the place and would give us a good price.'

'And?'

'Da said he'd have to think about it, and it's a bit awkward. He wants to get the contract for the new church, and Charlie Rattigan is on the committee who decides. Da reckons he has a big say in who is chosen.'

I thought of the night the Wren Boys stopped me and what Rats had said to Mattie about his father.

'That explains why he wanted you to invite him to the party.'

'Exactly. Isn't it the last thing we need – to be beholden to the Rattigans? Think of the power it'll give Rats! To be fair to Da, he said he would never put us under pressure to sell the place. But it *is* a tricky situation. Da wants to keep on Charlie's good side. Getting that contract would be a dream come true for him.'

I felt torn, thinking about my own da and what he would gain, but I couldn't say that to Redzer.

We walked up Cuffe Street and Kevin Street into the Coombe. Soon we were in Garden Lane, hiding behind a pony and cart. A few minutes later, a door opened and out came Darby, followed by Albertha. Darby grunted at her to hurry up. The menace in his voice struck fear into the pair of us. We stood still, hardly breathing as the pair passed within a few feet of us. They made their way towards Francis Street. A man on the street stopped Darby. We had to hide around the corner while they talked. We heard Darby's deep voice say 'Daniel O'Connell', but we couldn't make anything else out. Keeping hidden and quiet was tricky until we came to Dame Street. Here more people were out and about, especially around the newspaper office belonging to *Saunders's News-letter*. No doubt they were getting ready for the Dublin Tradesmen, who were to march through the streets later today and make a presentation to Daniel O'Connell at his house. A busier street made it easier to keep Darby and Albertha in view without being seen.

They swung around the corner into Nassau Street and used a side entrance to Trinity College. A porter at the gate ushered them through. They must have been given a job in the college. This was a surprise! One of the professors was a member of that society against boys being used to climb chimneys. Not having a chimney-cleaning machine, we hadn't been given a job there in over a year.

'I know the system in the college from listenin' to my brothers,' I told Redzer. 'They use the soot to fertilise the Fellows' Garden. We should wait there for Albertha to come out.'

We waited until the porter was distracted by a pony and trap going through the gate. When he stopped to talk to the driver, we scrambled in the far side, making our way up the short lane into the garden.

'It will be at least half an hour before she'll be down with the first sack. It depends where the chimney is in the college and how recently it's been cleaned.'

There was a garden seat off one of the paths. We sat down, but it was too cold to stay still, so we walked in the dark. Up the sides and down the middle we paced.

I pointed to a spot in one of the corners. 'This is where she'll be takin' the soot.'

The world was waking up. Lights twinkled in the windows. Half an hour had gone by. Where was Albertha? For the umpteenth time, we traipsed up the path closest to the high hedge until we heard somebody clearing their throat. We froze. Footsteps in the gravel told us the person was near.

Redzer grabbed my arm and whispered, 'It's a man. Is it Darby?'

But the man hadn't a sack. He wore a cloak and shuffled down the main path, talking to himself.

'The Lord is my Shepherd, there is nothing I shall want,' he said.

'He's sayin' his prayers,' I whispered. 'It must be one of those professors.'

The man continued down the path with his back to us now.

Somebody else turned the corner. Somebody carrying a sack of soot.

'Albertha,' I called in a loud whisper. She dropped the sack and moved over beside us. 'It's my friend and me. There's a man at the other end of the garden who might see us. We'll stay here 'til he's gone.'

We all ducked behind the hedge. The man came back up the middle path again, praying louder now. Albertha put her hand over her mouth, and I didn't know what she was doing until she took a fit of coughing.

'Hulloo,' said the professor, swinging around in our direction. 'Who's there?'

'Stay here,' whispered Albertha. We stayed crouched behind the hedge.

'It's only me, sir,' she said. 'I'm emptying the sack of soot from the chimney cleaning.' She grabbed the sack and emptied it quickly.

The professor came closer. 'You look like you've been up the chimney yourself, boy.'

'I have, sir.'

'And who, might I ask, employed you to do that? There was an agreement between all staff not to use climbing boys.'

'I only clean the chimneys, sir. I don't take note of who's

payin' the sweeper. You'll have to ask him.'

'Hmm. I will, indeed. Show me the way, boy.'

He marched her out of the garden and around the corner into a square. They walked across towards a building on the far side. We followed at a safe distance behind.

'Oh no, look!' I whispered to Redzer. Darby's face appeared at one of the windows on the first floor. He pulled the window up.

'Where are you going with my apprentice?' he shouted at the man below.

'To find out who hired you to do the job,' the professor shouted.

'The only person I have to answer to is the man payin' me,' said Darby. 'And it isn't you, so let go of my boy!'

Another window opened. A man stuck his head out and looked down. 'What's all this shouting?'

It was at that moment I spotted another way out of the square. It was our chance to bolt.

'Let's go!'

I started running past the professor and Albertha. Redzer followed me, and Albertha dropped the sack and followed us.

'Come back here, you ruffians!' shouted the professor.

But we were on our way towards the gate that led out to Great Brunswick Street. The further and faster we got away from Darby Madden, the better.

Chapter Fifteen

Breaking Free

'Stop! Let me catch my breath,' said Albertha once we had turned into Great Brunswick Street.

She leaned against the wall of the nearest house. I supposed there was no harm in taking a minute's rest.

'My name is Hugh,' I told Albertha, 'and this is my friend Owen.'

'When I heard your voice in the garden, I thought I was dreamin',' she said. 'I can't tell you how happy I am to see you. Where are we off to next?'

'We're goin' to the house of Signor Sapio further down this street. Izzy, the maid there, said you can clean up and change in the dairy out back.'

'And then?'

'We'll go to the police station and report Darby and afterwards to –'

'Come back here, boy!'

'Oh no!' shrieked Albertha, looking behind us. 'It's him!'

Darby was running after us.

'Quick, this way!' I started running down Great Brunswick

Street, the others following.

Ahead of us on our right was the Adelphi Theatre. A man stood out on the footpath, talking to an apple-woman. As we came nearer, I could see it was Paddy, the man Albertha and I had met that night at the back of the theatre. Should I ask him for help? Behind him, the door of the theatre was open.

'If I were you, I'd take my cart and do my sellin' up around Merrion Square, Sally,' he was saying to the apple-woman. 'There'll be thousands of people around to buy those gorgeous apples. Mother of God, what have we here?'

'Help us, Paddy!' I said as we came towards him.

Giving Darby a sharp look, Paddy quickly got a sense of what was happening,

'Ah, yez have finally arrived! In yez go, boys,' he said, standing to one side to let us in. He added in a whisper, 'Stand behind the door.'

Darby tried to follow us, but Paddy blocked the way.

'No admittance except on business,' said Paddy.

'Then why did you let those boys in ahead of me?' asked Darby.

'To help with the props. They've every right to be let in.'

'You're makin' that up. One of them's my climbin' boy. I saw him plainly with my two eyes!'

'Then listen plainly with your two ears, mister. You're not gettin' in.'

I couldn't see, but I imagined Paddy standing in the doorway like a giant stone pillar.

'I don't need the likes of you to advise me,' said Darby. We could hear his temper beginning to rise.

'And we don't need the likes of you around here, nor do those children. You better get yourself off, if you've any sense,' said Paddy.

'I could run down to the station for a constable,' said Sally.

'Will you, Sal? I'll look after your cart here 'til you come back,' said Paddy.

'Now, now, let's not get hasty,' said Darby. 'But tell that no-good climbin' boy of mine, he'll not get away that easily.'

There was silence for a minute. Darby seemed to have gone on his way.

Sally was the first to speak. 'The cheek of some people. Wouldn't blame those children for runnin' away from him.'

'Will you watch the door for me for a minute, Sally?' Paddy stepped into the hall. 'Nasty piece of work comin' after yez, boys! I'd advise yez to stay clear of Great Brunswick Street. Yez haven't seen the last of that fella yet. Cross the lobby here and go down through the theatre to the stage. There's another door on the left-hand side into a corridor. Keep going to the end – as far as the door out to the lane. Off with yez now.'

That was the lane at the back of Signor Sapio's house. We thanked Paddy and entered the theatre. It was in complete darkness, and there was a smell of tobacco and damp wool.

My hands brushed the side of the seats along the aisle towards the stage. I opened a door into a corridor, and we felt our way towards the end.

'I hope the key is in the door,' I said to the others.

We passed wooden crates, broken chairs, and a heap of old curtains. Finally, we came to the door, but no key.

'What'll we do?' asked Redzer.

'I'll have to go back and ask Paddy how we get out,' I said.

'Wait! Remember the night you chased me down the lane?' said Albertha. 'Paddy unlocked a door and hung the key on a hook. Maybe there's one for this door too?'

We searched each side of the door, and there it was, a key dangling from a hook.

'Got it! Good thinkin', Albertha!' I turned it, the door opened, and we could see the carriage lane ahead of us. We all tumbled out, and I locked the door and shoved the key back under it.

'Signor Sapio's is the fifth one down,' I said.

I lifted the latch on the gate, and we tiptoed through the garden. I pointed out the woodshed and the dairy to Albertha.

'These are some clothes of my sister's,' said Redzer shyly, handing her the bundle.

'Izzy also left some stuff. We weren't sure what would fit you.'

'Did someone say my name?'

'Izzy, here's Albertha,' I said.

'Come on, girl,' said Izzy kindly. 'Let's get you cleaned up.'

'We'll wait out on the carriage lane until you're ready.'

Figaro came running out to us, and we played with him, throwing sticks to fetch and walking him up and down the lane. I knew from climbing chimneys that it would take some time for Albertha to get cleaned up. She shyly came forward when she was finished. We stared at her. Was this the same person? She looked so much like a girl! All the soot and dirt were gone from her face, and her hands were red from scrubbing them clean. She had put on Izzy's clothes and Nancy's cloak and woollen cap. A few strands of blonde hair peeped out in front. She even walked like a girl!

'I haven't used warm water or soap since I left home,' she said as she and Izzy carried out plates with warm scones. 'I feel like a new person.'

'You look like a new person,' said Redzer, and we laughed.

There was jam in the scones and melting butter. Izzy popped into the dairy and came out with three cups of milk.

'Aunt Honorah's gone to the market, so we don't have to worry about her! There's always so much to eat and drink here. I doubt Signor Sapio would object to parting with some of it for such a good cause.'

There was one scone left. We gave it to Albertha. She was so thin and devoured the food eagerly; she was obviously starving. I licked the runny jam off my fingers and told Izzy where we were heading next.

'And after the police station, we're going to the House of Mercy in Baggot Street.'

'What's that?' asked Albertha.

'It's a place for homeless women and girls,' said Izzy. 'I heard the women who run it are very kind. They'll look after you.'

'Will they help me get home – to Belfast?' asked Albertha.

'I've no doubt they will,' said Izzy.

'And if you don't want to go there, you can stay in the hut in Harmony Yard,' said Redzer.

'I've got to go back now,' said Izzy. 'Good luck! Let me know how it all goes.'

'I promise I will,' I said.

We made our way towards College Street. The streets were filling up with people, but it wasn't the usual Tuesday-morning crowd. Splashes of bright colour popped up among the drab blacks and greys. Three men passed us wearing green and orange scarves. They had silver 'O'Connell' medals hanging from ribbons around their necks.

'That's some of the Tradesmen heading over to Swan's Hotel on the quays,' said Redzer. 'They'll be marching up to Daniel O'Connell's house later.'

We had to dodge a jaunting car on the street; the driver, wearing a huge green and orange rosette, was distracted by all the hustle and bustle around him. A man held a boy up on his shoulders to tie green ribbons on the lower branches of a tree. The police station across from Trinity College wasn't far away now. Once more, we passed the gate into the college, but we didn't get any further – Darby Madden came up from behind and grabbed Albertha's arm.

'Where do you think you're going?'

'Ow!'

'You're coming this way.'

'I'm not going with ye.'

'Let her go!' I shouted.

'We'll report you. We're going to the police station,' said Redzer.

'More like I'll report you,' said Darby. He shook Albertha roughly by the arm. 'I paid good money for you, and you haven't repaid your debt to me.'

'I don't owe you anything!' shouted Albertha.

But Darby dragged her by the arm the opposite way. Redzer and I walked fast beside Albertha. A minister and his wife coming toward us stopped talking to each other when they saw Darby's rough treatment.

'Excuse me, you're hurting that child,' said the minister.

'Excuse me, it's nothing to do with you.' Darby mimicked his accent.

'How dare you speak to my husband in that tone of voice?' said the woman.

I tried to pull Albertha away, but Darby's big hand gripped her arm. He wasn't going to let go that easily. He stopped and, with his free hand, gave me a mighty shove. I stumbled backwards, lost my balance and fell onto the street.

'Scholar!' Redzer's face was standing over me. 'Are you alright?'

I felt the back of my head: blood. A white hankie appeared in front of me. It was held by the minister's wife.

'I saw what that man has just done! Put that on your cut. We're going after him.'

I took it, thanked her, and pressed it to my throbbing head. The white hankie soaked up the blood.

'Now we've lost Albertha,' I cried, sitting up. Everything we had done was for nothing. My head throbbed, and inside I felt hollow and hopeless. Then a woman's singing voice filled the street.

O people of Erin, a garland entwine,
The shamrock, the laurel and roses combine,
For our hero O'Connell, whose soul is divine,
For saving old Ireland, in glory, he'll shine

Redzer and I looked at each other. We knew that voice!

'Bessie!' I shouted. 'Help!'

She pushed through the crowd and came face to face with us, the basket of herrings balancing on her head.

'Scholar, what's goin' on here?'

'Darby Madden pushed me.'

'Pushed you? What was that about?'

'We were trying to save a friend of ours – a girl – and he's taken her away.'

'Which way?'

I pointed in the direction.

'Quick, up. Let's go.'

She charged forward, the basket on her head.

Down the street, the minister had stopped Darby again.

Bessie stood beside them. 'Excuse me, Reverend. I need a word with this man.'

'What are you talking about?' said Darby. 'Never saw you in my life.'

'But I've seen *you*. You're the fella that was stayin' in McGinn's. What gives you the right to push this young lad into the street?'

'I don't have to answer to the likes of you,' said Darby. 'Get away from me.'

But Bessie wasn't going anywhere. 'And what about this girl? What's goin' on here?'

'I'm trying to establish that myself,' said the minister.

A couple of fishwomen, with baskets of cockles strapped to their backs, stopped and stood behind Bessie. Sally joined them with her apple cart.

'I'm glad you are, Reverend, because this brute should be nowhere next nor near children,' said Bessie.

'Keep your nose out of this,' said Darby in a low snarl.

'Did yez hear that?' said Bessie to the women behind her.

'He thinks I'm the kind of woman to stand by and do nothin'!' Her face was red with vexation.

'You're far from that, Bessie,' said Sally.

'First, he abuses his climbin' boy, then he pushes an innocent young boy into the street, and now he has his sights set on this girl.'

'Yeah, I saw him at the Adelphi earlier – chasin' children, he was,' said Sally. 'Wasn't it you two and another boy?' she asked me.

'I was the –' started Albertha.

'Hold your tongue!' shouted Darby, pulling at Albertha's arm. 'I'm in charge of the girl, and I don't have to explain anythin' to any of you.'

'We're not askin' you to explain,' shouted Bessie. 'It's clear to every man, woman and child standing here that these children are no concern of yours.'

'Hear, hear,' said the minister.

'You're wrong! The girl's my concern. I'm her guardian,' said Darby.

'Don't listen to him, missus,' cried Albertha. 'He's nothin' to me.'

'She's right, Bessie,' I said, holding Albertha's other arm. 'We're makin' sure the girl's safe.'

'I think we should call a policeman,' said the minister. More people were gathering around.

'Get your filthy hands off that child!' shouted Bessie at

Darby. 'You've no right to be draggin' her off.'

Two barefoot boys pushed forward out of the crowd. One was Joe Melody, Dexie's friend, and I didn't recognise the other.

'Scholar?' said Joe. 'Are y'alright? Heard you were being pushed around.'

'Scholar's alright, Joe,' said Bessie. 'It's the girl who needs help. Now let go!' she ordered, stepping in front of Darby.

'Get out of my way or you'll regret it, you old fishwife!' shouted Darby.

'Ah, here,' said one of the fishwomen behind Bessie. 'There's no need for that.'

'Sally!' shouted Bessie.

Sally plucked an apple from her cart and flung it full force at Darby, hitting him on the forehead. All the people standing around held their breaths, waiting to see what would happen next.

'Joe, take over,' said Bessie.

Joe stepped in front of Darby, who was dazed by the apple's force, and pushed him in the chest.

'That's for pushing my friend's brother!' he shouted. The other boy slipped in behind Darby and jumped up on his back. Such was the shock this gave him that he let go of Albertha. The crowd that had gathered around us in the street clapped and cheered.

'Don't ever threaten a Dublin fishwoman, mister,' said

Bessie. 'Go, go, children! Get away from the brute.'

'You haven't heard the end of this!' shouted Darby, trying to get the boy off his back.

'Neither have you, ya long streak o' misery!' shouted Bessie. 'We'd throw more apples, only we wouldn't waste good ones on a bad one like yourself!'

I didn't stop to thank Bessie. That could be done another time. We kept a fast pace going until we reached the police station. A grey-haired man with a huge moustache peered at us over a high desk.

'Is Constable Beardwood here, please?' asked Redzer.

'He's not here at the moment,' said the constable. 'Can I help you?'

Redzer hesitated. He knew Constable Beardwood and trusted him. That was all part of the plan.

'We really need to see him. When will he be back?'

'He's on duty over at Merrion Square and should be back by four o'clock.'

'Thank you, sir.'

We moved away from the desk.

'I think we should go over to Merrion Square and talk to him there,' said Redzer. 'First, check and see if there is any sign of Darby outside.'

I stepped out cautiously onto the path and checked in both directions. 'No sign.'

We crossed the road and passed by the main entrance to

Trinity College. Crowds were gathering. There was laughter and merriment around us, but we were on our guard now, each on the alert in case Darby came up again suddenly. We walked down Nassau Street. I knew I wouldn't feel easy until we spoke to Constable Beardwood. I calculated how long it should take us to get there and crossed my fingers that we'd have the good luck to get talking to him straight away.

Chapter Sixteen

Merrion Square

Droves of people thronged the streets to watch the Tradesmen march past on their way to present their address to Daniel O'Connell. Once I saw the crowds, I knew it would be impossible to speak to Constable Beardwood before the event. We had to push our way into Merrion Square. The gates of the park in the square, usually locked, had been opened for the occasion. Hundreds of people were inside the railings; many had climbed up into the trees.

'How on earth will we find Constable Beardwood?' asked Redzer.

'Can't we climb a tree ourselves?' I said. 'Albertha and I climb for a livin', don't forget.'

'Good idea,' said Redzer. 'Two out of the three of us know what the constable looks like.'

We squeezed through a gate and made our way to one of the trees that still had some space to offer and hoisted ourselves up. Although we could see over the crowd, we couldn't move to keep warm, and soon all three of us sat shivering among the branches. Most of the policemen were up at the front, making sure there was space left near Daniel O'Connell's house for the Tradesmen to gather.

'All these people are here to see Daniel O'Connell?' asked Albertha, surprised.

'Of course,' I said, wondering why she'd even have to ask the question.

'Is that you up there, Owen Lampkin?' came a voice below us. 'And Hugh O'Dare too!'

It was Brother Maloney. He was with Charlie Rattigan.

'Good morning, boys,' said Charlie. He looked at Albertha, trying to determine whether or not she was with us.

'I'm delighted to see you boys here,' said Brother Maloney.

'And this is a friend of ours, Albertha,' I said, and both men nodded 'hello' to her.

'We're heading closer to the front,' said Brother Maloney. 'James is keeping a place for us.'

He whispered some words to Charlie and spoke to us again. 'Why don't you come up with us?'

Although joining Rats wasn't a choice I'd normally make, it was our chance to get up close to the front near the policemen. It would also mean having a better place to see and hear Daniel O'Connell speak and a chance to move around to keep warm.

'Yes,' I answered. 'Thanks, Brother.'

We all climbed down and followed Charlie Rattigan and Brother Maloney. So many people had squeezed into the square we had to push hard to get through.

'Why did you call that man "brother"?' whispered Albertha.

'That's how you talk to a Christian Brother,' I whispered back. Being a girl, she may not have ever had dealings with them, I thought as she looked at me blankly. Soon we found ourselves moving through the crowd closest to the front, where men with armbands conducted people to different spaces.

'These three children are with us,' said Brother Maloney.

Rats and Francis were surprised – and not in a good way – when they saw us coming towards them. They reluctantly made space for us.

'We were being shown to a spot further back,' Rats told his father, 'but I complained to one of the stewards – told him who my father was – and he moved us up here.'

'Good boy. That was smart thinking,' said Charlie.

'I didn't realise you'd be bringing company,' said Rats, lowering his voice.

'Brother Maloney invited them,' said Charlie quietly. He turned around and started chatting to the grown-ups on the far side of him, introducing Brother Maloney. They were out of earshot now, a golden opportunity for Rats to get in some smart comments.

'We're in great company now, Francis. A manure yard boy, a climbing boy, and who's this you have with you?' said Rats, pointing to Albertha.

'Nobody you know,' I said. *Keep it civil*, I said to myself.

'Probably wouldn't *want* to know,' said Francis, and they both laughed.

Albertha scowled. 'The feeling's mutual,' she said.

Rats didn't look happy – he hadn't expected her to answer. But now we were all distracted by the noise coming from Baggot Street. The clapping and cheering swelled as the first Tradesmen entered Merrion Square. A man on a grey horse was leading them, wearing a silk sash on which 'The Trades of Dublin' was embroidered.

'That's Marcus Costello. He's the spokesman for the Tradesmen,' said Charlie Rattigan, shouting to be heard over the crowd. Behind Marcus Costello, the Tradesmen marched in rows of three; in each row, two men carried a trade banner, and a third walked beside them. Brush makers, painters, weavers, bookbinders, horseshoers, basket makers, skinners, hatters – we were dizzy reading all the banners that passed us by.

'That's my favourite,' said Albertha, pointing to the bricklayers. Two men carried a green silk banner with an Irish harp in the middle and a fringe of gold and silver. 'The harp on it reminds me of home. We've a harp society in Belfast.'

'I like the carpenters' banner best,' said Redzer.

'You'll be with them someday,' I told him.

Rats and Francis were sniggering at the motto on the tailors' banner: 'I was naked, and you clothed me.'

'Show a bit of respect,' said Albertha. 'That's a quotation from scripture.'

Francis made a face at her; Rats pretended he hadn't heard.

'What are they all marchin' for?' asked Albertha.

'To show support for Daniel O'Connell,' I explained. 'Now that he's a member of parliament, he wants to end the union of Ireland and Great Britain.'

'End the union?' repeated Albertha, scowling.

'Daniel O'Connell believes the union hasn't been good for Ireland, and that's why he wants to end it,' continued Redzer. 'And the Tradesmen support him. You saw some of them holding "Repeal the Union" banners?'

'I did. What does "repeal" mean?' asked Albertha.

'To get rid of the union – to change the law that unites the two countries,' I answered. 'The Tradesmen believe business would be better for them if a parliament in Dublin were in charge. They feel they'd be better looked after.'

Albertha muttered something under her breath. It sounded like, 'I wouldn't be so sure about that.'

It took almost half an hour for all the men to assemble. The thunderous sound of clapping and cheering filled the square. Daniel O'Connell had appeared on the balcony wearing a black coat and blue pantaloons. His blue travelling cap had a green and orange border, and a medal hung from a green and orange ribbon around his neck.

Everyone went quiet as the speeches began.

'Good God,' said Albertha, louder than she ought to. 'It's the Bully Beggarman himself.'

'Shhh!' I said to her. What was she thinking, saying something like that?

'Did you hear that?' said Rats. 'Did you hear what that girl called our great leader, our Liberator?'

'Take that back, girl,' said Francis. 'How dare you insult our hero?'

'Call him whatever ye want, but that's what we call him in Belfast.'

'You're not in Belfast now,' said Rats, 'so mind your tongue.'

'Don't look so shocked,' said Albertha to me. 'We've no time for Daniel O'Connell where I come from, and that's the nickname we gave him.'

I *was* shocked. No time for the Liberator? Giving him horrible nicknames? I started trying to think of the best way to reply. 'Well, I ...'

'You've your way of seein' things, and we've ours,' continued Albertha. 'I'll not say anythin' else except we're very *loyal* to the union in Belfast.'

'Belfast!' said Francis. 'That reminds me of Stephen's night and that boy we met.'

I didn't know what they meant by this, but Albertha turned to them, her face like thunder. 'Oh, does it now?'

'Shh,' said Charlie Rattigan to her. 'The speeches are starting.'

Marcus Costello appeared on the balcony with his address to Daniel O'Connell in his hand. He opened the scroll and started to read. 'On your return to Ireland, the Tradesmen of Dublin offer a warm welcome to Ireland's great Liberator.'

The crowd went mad, clapping and whooping.

'Your dearest wish is our dearest wish: to have our own parliament back in Dublin.'

Again, the crowd went into a frenzy of cheering.

Marcus Costello continued with his speech and finished almost in tears. 'May the Almighty, the giver of all blessings, lengthen your days in happiness that you may long live to see Ireland as she ought to be, "Great, glorious and free, first flower of the earth and first gem of the sea". Signed on behalf of the Tradesmen of Dublin.'

There was thunderous applause again. The end of the speech reminded me of that verse Bessie Reilly had handed me on Sunday evening. Marcus Costello rolled up the scroll he had read and presented it to Daniel O'Connell.

It was now the Liberator's turn to speak. He thanked the Tradesmen for their kindness and talked about the terrible loss of the Irish Parliament thirty years ago when the Act of Union was passed. 'That evil union has destroyed our manufacturers and our businesses; it has robbed our labourers of work, ruined our farmers and caused thousands of able-bodied workers to leave our native land. What has caused the richest land to be covered with the poorest people on the face of the earth? The answer is obvious: the union with Great Britain. Let us never be easy until we succeed in ending the union and setting up our own parliament again in Dublin.'

There was more loud clapping and applause. Daniel O'Connell reminded his listeners that he was not in favour of violence. He advised people to obey the law and be 'quiet and peaceable'. I loved the way he spoke; I felt as if he were talking to me on my own. And I loved the way he said that every person in the square at this presentation mattered. He wasn't just saying words – he really cared. He finished with three cheers for the king and three for old Ireland.

Redzer and I cheered heartily. Men took off their hats and waved them, and women waved their hankies.

'There's Constable Beardwood!' said Redzer, pointing to the corner of Merrion Square and Fitzwilliam Street. 'We've got to go.'

We said goodbye to Brother Maloney and Charlie Rattigan, who were curious about why we needed to speak to a constable. But we gave nothing away.

Albertha said something to Rats and Francis as she passed them. I couldn't hear it, but going by Rats's face, I could tell whatever was said unnerved him. Francis stared at her, his mouth slightly open. The square emptied the way a busy schoolyard clears within seconds once the bell for class is rung.

When we approached Constable Beardwood and told him we needed to talk to him, he beckoned us to follow him downstairs to the kitchen in Mr O'Connell's house.

'This looks serious,' he said curiously.

'It is serious, sir, and we specially looked for you to report to,' said Redzer.

'Before you tell me anything, please let me sit down,' Constable Beardwood said. 'My legs are going to collapse. I've been standing there since ten o'clock this morning.'

Constables, maids and ushers scurried around the table in the steam-filled kitchen. Mrs Sullivan's face was among the crowd, and she came over to us. 'I hope these young scamps aren't in trouble.'

'They're not, but would it be alright if we stepped into your scullery for a few minutes? It's so busy in the kitchen, and I need to talk to these three.'

'Of course it would, as long as you don't mind that I'm in there too. I'm still catching up on my work.'

Redzer looked at Albertha to see if she was alright with that, and then we all went into the scullery, a cool and calm little room. Constable Beardwood pulled out a stool that was under the sink. We three sat on a narrow bench, and Mrs Sullivan stood cutting meat and onions at the table at the other wall with her back to us.

The policeman took out a jotter and a pencil and opened the first page. 'You've a story that you want me to hear, I believe?' he said to Albertha.

'I have, sir,' said Albertha.

Chapter Seventeen

The Story

'I grew up in Belfast,' said Albertha. 'My ma's a mill worker; so was her ma b'fore her. There's only her and me. Never knew my daddy. Last summer, she became ill. At first, we weren't worried – we were hopin' it'd pass. But come September, she was gettin' weaker. The sickness was that bad, she couldn't go to work some days.'

'Where did she work?' asked Constable Beardwood.

'Mulholland's on York Street – as a spinner. With days missed, less money was comin' into the house, but the rent still had to be paid. I wanted to work, but my earnings wouldn't have been enough. That's why Ma decided to send me down to her sister in Mullingar.'

'She didn't consider going herself?'

'Ma said my uncle wouldn't put up with the two of us arrivin' on the doorstep. We couldn't afford the coach fare, but a neighbour of ours knew of a man bringin' bales of linen down to Belvedere House, near Mullingar, and he could give me a lift.'

'Belvedere House' was written on the jotter.

'When I think back on that day, leavin' my mother and

climbin' into that wagon, I can hardly believe what's happened to me since, but I'll try to tell you as best I can.'

'Can you remember the date?' asked Constable Beardwood.

'Yes. It was the sixteenth of October – the day before I turned twelve.'

The policeman noted the date. 'Please continue.'

'The man was called Sam Millar. We left Belfast, and it seemed like an eternity before we got to Banbridge. We were drivin' through the town when a man stopped us and asked us if we were going to Dundalk. He was looking for a lift. Sam wasn't on for bringin' him at first – the cart was so full – but the man offered to pay him, and he decided to take him.'

She stopped for a minute, and Mrs Sullivan stopped cutting the meat and onions at the far table.

'He was all chat, askin' me where I came from and where I was goin'. Said his name was Danny, but now I think that could've been made up. He seemed friendly and kept chattin' as we went along.'

'Did he tell you what his business was in Dundalk?'

'He said he had to meet a couple of friends there. After that, he was goin' to Dublin to board a ship for America. I could scream when I think of what I told him. How fooled I was by him being friendly. We stopped in Dundalk. Sam had to collect some goods and said if I wanted to get some food or somethin' to drink, now was the time. He said he'd meet me back at the horse and cart at three o'clock.'

'Can you remember whereabouts in Dundalk you stopped?'

'I think it was called Bridge Street. Then Danny said he had the money to buy me a bowl of soup in one of the eatin' houses. I was ravenous and was only too delighted to go with him. We went into this place – can't remember the name – and he ordered a bowl of soup for me. While I was tuckin' in, he talked to a tall man up at the counter. The two of them looked over at me, but I thought Danny was just tellin' him he was treatin' me, and I didn't think anythin' of it. By the time I finished my soup, Danny was gone, and the tall man came down to me. That man was Darby Madden.

'"There's been a change of plan," he told me. "You're to finish your journey with me."

'"I'd rather go with Sam, thank you," I said.

'"Who's Sam?" he asked.

'"The man I came with – the driver of the cart."

'"He's gone."

'"He can't be," I said and stood up. "It's not gone three o'clock."

'"Let's go back then and see if I'm right."

'He walked with me to the yard where Sam Millar had left his horse and cart, and there was no sign of it. I couldn't believe it.

'"I think I'll try and go back home," I said to him.

'That's when he grabbed my wrist and said, "You'll go with me, girl. I'm a chimney sweeper in need of a climbing boy, and you'll do for that."

"'I'll not climb any chimney," says I, "and I'll shout for help if you don't let me go."

"'And I'll tell of how you were abandoned, and I took you on and how you stole from me. Fancy going to Australia as a convict? Shout, and that's what'll happen."

"'Then I'll tell them the truth about what you did," I said.

"'Your word against mine?" said Darby. "You wouldn't stand a chance. What's your name?"

'I wouldn't tell him at first, but I was so upset and scared I told him in the end.'

'Your full name is?' asked Constable Beardwood.

'Albertha McCoy.'

'Please continue.'

"'Your name will be Bert from now on," Darby told me. "I'll not be listenin' to a bunch of well-to-do women whinin' about me taking on a climbin' girl."

'He brought me to a horrible lodgin' house, cut my hair, and swapped my clothes for dirty trousers, a scruffy jacket and a cap. Needless to say, we weren't goin' anywhere near Mullingar. It was to Dublin we were headin'. I saw Sam's cart ahead of us on the road out of town. I ran after it, callin' for Sam to stop, and Darby stood laughin' at me. The man who was drivin' Sam's cart turned around. It was Danny! He tipped his hat and kept goin'. Whatever happened to poor Sam Millar, I do not know.

'Darby got us a lift in a cart full of animal skins. The smell of it turned my stomach, not to mention the cold and fear I felt on that journey. For the first few weeks, we lodged in Montgomery Street. Darby taught me the different ways to climb and use the scraper and the brush. I often had to sleep on my sack with another sack around me for a blanket. I had sores on my knees and elbows.'

'What about food?' asked Constable Beardwood.

'Aye, food. Always plenty for himself and little or nothin' for me. Said he wanted to keep me small to get up the chimneys. Had to steal at the market sometimes, or I'd have starved.'

'Good God,' said the policeman. He was so absorbed in the story he had stopped writing. 'I've heard a lot in my day, but this is really shocking. Can you describe Darby Madden to me?'

'Very tall, black hair, his nose is kind of crooked, probably broken at some stage.'

'He has an accent from one of the Ulster counties,' I added. 'Not sure which one.'

'Thank you. Now continue with your story.'

'When work was dryin' up on the north side of town, we came to this side and rented the cellar from Mrs McGinn in Verschoyle Court. By then, I'd made up my mind to run away. Hugh knows about the first time. His uncle and brothers were tryin' to scare Darby and me out of the place, and I took my chance and ran.'

'Where did you go?'

'When I was runnin' away from Hugh, I ran into that street in front of Trinity College. Then I ventured further on my own. I asked people where the road to Belfast was, but nobody would answer me. Then I met a gang of Wren Boys. Thought they'd be good to ask, and I did. Sure enough, they told me the way to go. But before they let me go, they asked me if I had any money. To tell you the truth, I had one penny in my pocket, but I wasn't going to part with that.

'"I don't have any," I told them.

'"I wouldn't believe a lyin' climbin' boy," said one. He knocked me over, put his hand in my pocket and stole my last penny.

'"That'll teach you not to lie," he said, and he and the rest of the Wren Boys took off, leaving me lying on the street. I was starvin' and had to beg for food but got nothin' from nobody. I don't know how I did it, but I got up and went on my way, following the directions to the letter, but when I checked with someone else later if I was on the right road for Belfast, it turned out to be the road for Cork. I couldn't walk a step further between the cold and the hunger.'

Wren Boys? I thought to myself as Albertha spoke. *That has to be Rats and his gang.*

'You're saying that the Wren Boys told you the wrong road on purpose?' asked Constable Beardwood. 'Then robbed your money?'

'I am. I should have said *one* of the Wren Boys, and I had the bad luck to meet him again today in Merrion Square.'

'You met him again?' Constable Beardwood looked up from his notebook. 'Are you sure?'

'Certain. With or without a Wren Boy costume, I would recognise him anywhere. The boy's name is James Rattigan. The boys here call him "Rats". Rat by name, rat by nature, I'd say.'

Now it was clear what had happened between Rats and Albertha out in the square.

'Rattigan? Good God, Charlie Rattigan's son?' He wrote 'James Rattigan' in his notes. 'What happened next?'

'I was brought back.' Albertha stopped and laughed weakly. 'Would you believe that a man with a cart full of kindling brought me back? He recognised me and felt Darby should look after me and not leave me wanderin' the streets. I was too weak and hungry to say "no". Oh God, if only he knew!'

Albertha paused. Her lip quivered at this painful memory. Constable Beardwood looked kindly at the girl and waited for her to start again.

'We moved to Garden Lane that evenin' – Sunday evenin'.'

'Is that where Darby Madden is staying tonight?'

'He was plannin' to. Don't know if he's still there.'

'Go back to your story. You moved to Garden Lane …'

'Yes, I had the chance to ask Hugh for help yesterday.' She described how we met and how she wrote 'HELP' in the snow.

'Was that the time you found out she was a girl?' Constable Beardwood asked me.

I told him about St Stephen's Day and chasing Albertha down the theatre lane.

'Why didn't you tell your family what you had found out that evening?'

'I did, but they wouldn't believe me. They thought Darby's climbin' boy had made the story up – to make runnin' away easier.'

'I see. Continue now, Albertha,' said Constable Beardwood.

'Hugh made it his business to find out where we were workin' this mornin' – himself and Owen there.'

'Where was that?'

'Trinity College. One of the new professors got us to come in to clean his chimney. When I came out to empty the soot in the garden, the pair of them helped me escape. That was a kindness I'll never forget.'

'And then?'

'Darby came after me, but we got away. We ran down the street, and a wee girl Hugh knows called Izzy – who works as a maid at an Italian singing teacher's house – gave me food and clothes. We were followed by Darby once more, but thanks to this big strong fishwoman, we got away from him again.'

'I take it that's Bessie Reilly?' Constable Beardwood said to me.

'It is,' I told him.

'That gave us a chance to run up to the police station where we looked for you,' continued Albertha. 'We didn't see him after that.'

'Did you report him to any of the policemen there?'

Albertha shook her head, and I spoke up.

'We were so wary of Darby that we felt you were the only policeman we could trust. We were told you were on duty over here, so we made our way over. And here we are.'

A sound of sobbing came from the far table. Mrs Sullivan pulled a big white hankie out of her apron pocket and dabbed her eyes. 'Ah, you poor *cailín*. To think of all you went through. You won't leave my kitchen, *a leanbh*, 'til I've fed you. I've some stew left from earlier – enough for all of you.'

'That would be delightful, Mrs Sullivan,' said Constable Beardwood.

'I'd like nothin' better,' said Albertha, and Mrs Sullivan gave her a friendly pat on the back.

Chapter Eighteen

The Liberator

We were all given a bowl of lamb stew, and it was a sign of how hungry we were and how good it was that there wasn't a word spoken while we ate. When we were finished, Mrs Sullivan insisted we have a cup of tea and a slice of Christmas pudding. She asked one of the maids to serve us as she had to go up and check on 'the Master'.

'That was delicious,' said Constable Beardwood. 'I'd better get going. I must write a report on what you told me back at the station.'

He stood up to go, but one of the maids stepped forward. 'Mrs Sullivan said not to let you go before she talks to you. Would you mind waiting a minute, sir, and let me tell her you're about to leave?'

'Of course.'

Within minutes she was back with Mrs Sullivan, whose eyes were still red from crying.

'The Master wants to see you all above in his library,' she said. 'Will you come this way?'

We all followed her up the stairs. I found myself back in

the room where I had swept the chimney only a few days ago.

'Thank you, Mrs Sullivan,' said Mr O'Connell as his house-keeper brought us in. 'Will you check that Mrs O'Connell is alright in the drawing room? I've left her in charge of my visitors. Come in, come in, all of you.' He pointed to a long seat under the crucifix and a chair for the constable. 'Good afternoon, Constable. I have just been told a story by Mrs Sullivan that has utterly astounded me.'

He rose and walked around to stand in front of his desk. Up close, I couldn't take my eyes off his 'Order of Liberators' medal. 'I can see young Hugh admiring my medal. I may be known as the Liberator, but I have in this room two remark-able young liberators whom I wish to salute.'

He followed this with a salute to Redzer and me. I had to pinch myself that I wasn't dreaming. Here was Daniel O'Connell, who had just been watched by thousands of people, saluting the pair of us.

'And I am honoured to be in the presence of the girl they liberated.' He made a short bow to Albertha, then turned to the policeman. 'What do you make of it, Beardwood?'

'An extraordinary story, sir,' said the policeman. 'I'm head-ing back to the station to file a report. Our first action will be to check if the villain is still in Garden Lane.'

'Glad to hear it. That Madden man must be found and taken in. I remember Mrs Sullivan telling me about him on

Christmas Eve. To think the blackguard was standing on my own doorstep!'

He came over to me and shook my hand, then Redzer's. 'You two boys are to be congratulated on the way you orchestrated this girl's escape. You showed more courage and kindness than most grown-ups in my acquaintance.' He then took Albertha's hand and shook it. 'And you're to be commended for your bravery and smart thinking. What a clever idea to write "HELP" in the snow.'

'Thank you, sir,' said Albertha. Her cheeks turned bright red.

'And what a terrible ordeal you've been through. I could hardly believe my ears when Mrs Sullivan came in and told me your story. She's a tough woman from the wilds of the Black Valley in Kerry, and there she was, crying her eyes out over the hardship forced on you. Now, first things first. We need to contact your mother and aunt to tell them you're safe. I'll write to them both if you give me their names and addresses.'

'Thank you, sir. I can give you my aunt's address, but I'm not sure where my mother's livin' now or if she's ...' Two big tears ran down Albertha's cheeks. Daniel O'Connell pulled a hankie out of a drawer in his desk and pressed it into her hand. She patted her eyes. 'Not to hear a word from me or about me. I dread to think what that was like for her.'

'Poor girl. You've been through so much,' said Daniel O'Connell. 'Is there a priest or a minister I could write to?'

'Yes. I can give you the name and address of our minister.'

'Good. I'll get those letters written this evening.'

There was a knock at the door, and Mrs Sullivan looked in. 'Sorry to disturb you, sir, but the other girl has arrived.'

'Thank you, Mrs Sullivan. Will you send her in, please?'

In walked Izzy. Daniel O'Connell beamed at her. 'So, Signor Sapio got my note?'

'He did, sir, and sent me here in a cab straight away.'

'When I heard about your role in Albertha's rescue, I thought you must be sent for at once.'

Izzy looked around at us all and smiled.

'Take a seat there. Have you ever heard Signor Sapio mention the Society for Superseding the Necessity of Climbing Boys?'

'Often. Signor Sapio's a member and goes to all their meetings,' replied Izzy.

'You've never heard of it, Albertha?'

'No, sir.'

'The people in that society are trying their best to get chimney sweeps to use machines instead of climbing boys.'

'That's what that professor was talking about in the college,' said Albertha. 'The one who was cross to see climbin' boys being hired.'

'That was probably Doctor Singer. His brother Paul is a leading member of the society. I've no doubt they would like to hear your story and perhaps use it in their campaign. Would you be willing to let them tell it, Albertha?'

'I would,' she said. 'If I thought it would stop the likes of Darby Madden, I'd tell it a thousand times.'

'In that case, I think we should also contact the papers. They'd love this story for their readers. There's nothing like the papers to get the message out to people. I should know! I'll contact some journalists first thing in the morning.'

'Mr O'Connell,' said Redzer. 'My brother is working as a journalist for *The Dublin Newsletter.*'

'What's his name?'

'Mattie Lampkin.'

'Mattie Lampkin … Can't say I know him.'

'That's because he's always given boring stories about charity sermons and dinners,' said Redzer. 'This is the sort of story he really wants to write.'

'How long has he been with them?' asked Daniel O'Connell.

'Six months,' answered Redzer.

'I think he'd do a great job with it,' I chimed in. 'I know he was hopin' to write an article about the Dublin Anti-Slavery Society recently.' I thought it was better not to say that Mattie's boss thought he was too young to write it.

'Was he, indeed?' said Daniel O'Connell.

'If he's your brother, I would love him to write my story,' said Albertha to Redzer.

'That can all be arranged,' said Daniel O'Connell. 'Though I can tell you some of the older journalists' noses will be out of joint. But never mind that. The other papers can get in on the story the following day, which no doubt they will. This is the sort of story people are keen to read.'

He started shuffling a pile of papers on his desk. 'At least this one has a happy ending. Poor Bob O'Leary wasn't as lucky.'

'Bob O'Leary …' said Albertha sadly. 'When I heard how that wee boy died, I thought to myself, "that could be me". You'll not be surprised to hear that when Darby heard the news, all he did was shrug his shoulders and shout at me to carry on.'

'Banish those thoughts now, my dear. By the way, I wasn't impressed to hear that young Rattigan sent you on the wrong road and took your last coin,' he said. 'Wasn't impressed at all.'

'Excuse me, Mr O'Connell,' said the policeman. 'There's one further question I need to ask Miss McCoy. Where are you staying tonight?'

'Will you explain, Hugh?' she asked me.

'We were going to bring Albertha to the House of Mercy in Baggot Street or, if that wasn't what she wanted, to the hut in Harmony Yard.'

'That's kind of you, boys,' said Daniel O'Connell, 'but there are plenty of rooms in this house. There's a spare room next to Mrs Sullivan's that you could use until you go home, Albertha.'

She clapped her hands and laughed. 'When I heard about going to the House of Mercy, I didn't know what to think as I had never heard of one before. When I thought about the wee hut I might sleep in, I thought it'd be like a hotel compared to the places I've slept in over the last few months. But to sleep in a real bed in this house? Why, it'll be like a palace!'

Chapter Nineteen

The Story Gets Out

I walked up with Redzer and Izzy to Great Brunswick Street. Some stragglers from the meeting in Merrion Square still hung around, but most had gone home as requested by Daniel O'Connell.

'What a day. Mattie must have been surprised when he saw the straw and blankets left in the hut in Harmony Yard,' said Redzer.

'I think he'll be alright when he hears about the story we're givin' him,' I replied. 'You must have got a fright when Daniel O'Connell sent for you, Izzy?'

'Got a fright? I nearly fainted. My aunt gave the note to Signor Sapio when it arrived, so when I was summoned to the drawing room and saw him standing there with tears in his eyes, I didn't know what I was going to hear.'

'What did he say when he heard about the food and Albertha coming in to wash herself?'

'He was fine with it. The way he looked on it was that he helped Albertha, even though he didn't know it at the time.'

'And your aunt?'

'As I told you before, she has a kind heart, and that "cross housekeeper" face she has on most of the time was gone while she asked me about what had happened. In fact, my aunt suggested to Signor Sapio that I'd be sent around quickly in a cab! He agreed straight away, and I felt like a lady of quality being driven around to Merrion Square to the house of Daniel O'Connell.'

★ ★ ★

Da looked up from the fire when I walked in.

'Where on earth have you been all day? Tim said you left the house at some ungodly hour this morning.'

'I had to take care of somethin', and it took longer than expected.'

'Take care of what?' asked my mother.

'Remember Darby Madden ... the story I told you about his climbin' boy being a girl?'

'Not that again,' said Da.

'Let him talk, Bartle,' said Ma.

'I was right. She *is* a girl. Darby bought her from another man in Dundalk last October, and since then, he's made her work at the climbin'.'

'What?' said Da. 'Did you say "bought"? Start again and tell us the story from the beginnin'.'

So I told them, even the bits they knew already, like chasing

Albertha down the lane on Stephen's night and how she was brought back to Darby. I told them how she wrote 'HELP' in the snow and all about Trinity College this morning and how we ended up in Daniel O'Connell's house.

'When I think of Bessie coming in and tellin' us about how she was looking for the road to Belfast, I feel bad now,' said Ma.

'And I feel bad we didn't believe you, son,' said Da.

That evening, I had to repeat the whole story for my brothers and sisters.

'That's where you were going this mornin',' said Tim. 'I was goin' to follow you. Now I wish I did.'

* * *

We trudged down Stephen's Lane at four o'clock the following morning, our faces cut by the east wind blowing from the Irish sea. We had two jobs in Baggot Street. The first was Larry Bermingham's, the baker. That was a regular place for us, and Larry always sent us off afterwards with a couple of fresh loaves. After that, it was Ned McEvoy's. He made candles from tallow, and the smell of the animal fat would turn your stomach. Unlike Larry, Ned would never give anything away for free and was deeply suspicious of everyone. He followed us around for fear we would steal from him, and nothing would convince him otherwise.

We were finishing up in McEvoy's when Ned begrudgingly let one of the men who worked for Tom Lampkin into his kitchen.

'You're wanted in Lampkins',' he said, out of breath.

'Did somethin' happen?' I asked.

'No, it's Mattie. Wants to ask you questions for the paper.'

'Go on,' said Dexie. 'Join us later in O'Neill's in Mark Street.'

I ran to Lampkins', where Redzer met me at the door. 'Mattie's inside, and he's taking it all very seriously. Be prepared for lots of questions.'

'Did he talk to Albertha yet?'

'Spent two hours with her in Merrion Square this morning. Then he questioned me. Now you're for it.'

'Alright if I pop down to the scullery and wash my hands?'

'Go right ahead,' said Redzer.

When I finished, I made my way to the drawing room, where Mattie sat at the mahogany table. There were pages spread out all over, and he had a pencil poised and a jotter open. 'Sit down, Scholar, please.' His face was flushed with excitement.

I went through the whole story again about Albertha, but Mattie often stopped me and asked me questions like 'What was that like for you?' or 'What did you think might happen next?' He read out a piece that Albertha had told him and asked me if that was how I remembered what had happened. He also repeated part of Redzer's account and wanted to know if I needed to add anything.

I peeped into his notebook. It was all squiggles and marks.

'You're looking at my notes?' said Mattie.

'Yes – what way have you written them?'

'That's called "shorthand". Journalists use it to write down every word quickly.'

I was impressed, but I was even more curious to find out about Darby. 'Have you spoken to Constable Beardwood?' I asked.

'Yes, I was with him this morning.'

'Have they brought Darby in yet?'

'No, but the police are looking for him as we speak. He was too smart to go back to that place in Garden Lane.' He smiled. 'I'll have to hand it to yourself and Redzer – you were some pair to do what you did. And you should have been there to see the shock on my face when the editor called me into his office to tell me he wanted me to write about it!'

'They might start asking you to report on other stuff now,' I said.

'Hopefully they will, but thanks for this chance. I need to write up my story now and get it to my editor.'

I left the house and headed for Mark Street, but I had hardly walked a dozen steps when a man on the street stopped me. I had no idea who he was.

'Are you young Hugh O'Dare? One of the boys who saved that climbing girl?'

He insisted on shaking my hand. I was glad I had been able to wash it in Lampkins'!

I don't know how the story got around so fast, but I was stopped four more times on my way. One woman tried to bring me in to meet her family, but I told her I had to keep going. When I finally reached Mark Street, my brothers were coming out with their sacks.

'He must have asked you a hundred questions,' said Dexie, but I could see he wasn't annoyed with me. 'God knows we've been asked at least that many by everyone we met. We're going to Fortune's in Westland Row next, so you can follow us there.'

'Why can't I come with you now?'

'John O'Neill is upstairs waiting for you. He wants to talk to you.'

'To me?'

'He insists on hearin' the story "from the horse's mouth".'

I couldn't hide the surprise I felt. The cabinet maker was one of the quietest men we knew and, if anything, he avoided talking to people. 'How did he hear it?'

'He didn't say,' said Cricket. 'It didn't come from us, but everyone's talkin' about it.'

When I went upstairs, not only were John O'Neill and his wife waiting for me but Mr O'Hara, the dairyman, Mr Thacker, the bookbinder, and Miss McMinamy, the dressmaker. I felt like I was walking into a little audience in the parlour. I told my story, and afterwards Mrs O'Neill served tea and Christmas pudding and insisted that I have the first slice.

Mr O'Neill shook his head. 'Isn't that Darby fellow the very devil?'

Everyone agreed that they wanted him caught and punished.

Mr Thacker loved that we helped with Robinson Crusoe's boat at the pantomime. He sat up when I said it was Albertha's favourite story. 'I will make sure the young lady gets a copy of *Robinson Crusoe* this afternoon.'

'And shame on those Wren Boys for putting the poor child astray and stealing her last penny,' said Miss McMinamy. 'I heard Charlie Rattigan's young lad did it.'

'I heard the same,' said Mr Thacker.

'Anyway, she's being well looked after now,' said Mr O'Hara. 'From Mrs McGinn's cellar in Verschoyle Court to Merrion Square. That's some turnaround.'

'I wonder if the girl needs a new frock?' said Miss McMinamy. 'I could run up one for her at no charge.'

As I listened to the grownups talking, I wondered if they were trying to impress one another or were they in earnest about helping Albertha. A second slice of pudding appeared before me, placed there by Mrs O'Neill. She was very taken with the fact that Redzer and I were bold enough to enter Trinity College and hide in the Fellows' Garden.

'To think of all the years I've passed that place, and I never stood inside it – I'd never dare. And here, my two buckos were hiding behind the hedge!' she said.

Everyone agreed with her that Redzer and I were daring to try it.

This was the pattern of that day. I was stopped by street hawkers, shopkeepers, boys in my class, parents, and priests. I never made it in time for that job in Westland Row. When I got back home, the house was full of neighbours.

'Here he is,' said my sister Mary when I came to the door.

Everyone clapped as I walked in.

'Come in, son, come in,' said Da, standing up. 'The story has spread like wildfire.'

'You were talked about in Taylor's today,' said Mary. 'The Master and Missus were even askin' me, were you my brother.'

'What was it like in Mr O'Connell's house?' whispered Mrs Callan, who lived next door. 'Is it all green everywhere?'

'Will you leave the boy alone,' said my mother. 'He's exhausted. Did you get anythin' to eat, Scholar? I've a bit of dinner put by for you.'

I spoke words I thought I'd never hear myself say. 'I'm too full to eat anythin', Ma.'

'Hand it over here, Ma,' said Dexie. 'I'm not too full to eat it!' He took the plate and fork and started eating the potatoes, fried in dripping.

'I never saw so many people come to the house in one day,' said Ma. 'All lookin' for the O'Dare brothers to clean their chimneys. It's a pity you weren't here yourself, Hugh. We could have done with someone to write down all the names and addresses.'

'And every single last one heard about what you did,' said Da. 'And they –'

I didn't hear the end of that sentence. The words melted away as I drifted into a deep sleep in the corner.

Chapter Twenty

The True Story of Climbing Boy McCoy

The following morning, the sun was up by the time I woke.

'We decided to let you sleep in,' said Ma. 'The two lads said they'd manage today without you. And Redzer's been in and asked you to call over.'

Sauntering up Great Brunswick Street, I met Izzy on her way back from the grocer.

'You have saved me a journey,' she said when she saw me. 'Signor Sapio is looking for you.'

'I'm on my way to Lampkins' –'

'Don't worry, this won't take long. Someone else also wants to meet you.'

She brought me into a little sunny parlour at the front of the house. 'Here's Hugh O'Dare, sir.'

'I am so happy to meet you and shake your hand,' said

Signor Sapio, taking my hand and nearly shaking it off.

Brother Maloney was sitting on the opposite chair, and he hopped up too. 'My dear boy,' he said. 'You're the talk of the parish. We have all read Mattie's account in the *Dublin News-letter,* and we're not the better of it!'

'And my Isabella had a part to play in this story,' said Signor Sapio, pointing to the newspaper. It took a minute to realise he meant Izzy. 'A story that has touched the hearts of many people this morning.'

Izzy grinned. Signor Sapio continued. 'I would like to hold a concert to raise money for the little girl.'

'That's very kind of you, sir,' I said.

'Just what you'd expect from this generous man,' said Brother Maloney.

Signor Sapio bowed. 'I will talk to Mr Connello. I will go there now.'

'You mean Mr O'Connell, sir,' said Izzy. 'Hugh has to leave too. He was on his way to the Lampkins'.'

'To meet his friend. Very good. *Arrivederci,* young man.'

Brother Maloney cleared his throat. 'Hugh, before you go … I just wanted to say, I was taken aback when I heard what James Rattigan did. That day when you came to give me the message – I'm sorry I doubted what you told me.'

Now it was my turn to be taken aback. Brother Maloney apologising to *me*? 'That's alright, Brother,' was all I could think of saying.

'Could you wait just another minute?' asked Brother Maloney. 'Signor Sapio has arranged for someone else to meet you.'

I was anxious to get going, but I felt a few more minutes would be alright. Sure enough, Izzy appeared and announced the visitor: 'Mr Richard Webb.'

The tall man took off his hat and walked in.

'Good morning, all. Hugh O'Dare, I read your remarkable story in the newspaper this morning.'

'Sit down, *Ricardo,*' said Signor Sapio. Izzy took his coat, and he sat down. '*Mio amico* has come here with a purpose.'

'That's the Italian for "my friend",' said Mr Webb with a smile, and he began to talk. I listened carefully. When he finished, he shook hands with me. 'Not a word to anyone until you discuss it with your parents.'

I left with a light heart and a new secret.

★ ★ ★

Mattie nearly knocked me over, running out the door. 'Hugh! Sorry, I can't stop. Have to rush. The paper's in there on the table.'

There was a smell of fried rashers in the kitchen, and Mr Lampkin was sitting at the table reading out Mattie's article. 'Just in time, Hugh,' he said. He showed me the headline: 'The True Story of Climbing Boy McCoy'.

Mr Lampkin read out the account as if it were a play. He did our voices and made Albertha sound like she was from Belfast when he read what she said, and he even did a Kerry accent for Daniel O'Connell.

'I think my Mattie did a great job at the writing,' said Mrs Lampkin.

'He did indeed,' I agreed.

A knock at the kitchen door interrupted us. One of the maids from Daniel O'Connell's house was at the front door. 'Reporters are waiting to talk to Miss McCoy,' she said. We had to think for a minute who 'Miss McCoy' was. 'The Master asked if you could come over and answer some questions, too.'

'Isn't it hard to believe that it's us in the story?' I said to Redzer as we left for Merrion Square. 'I had to pinch myself listenin' to your da and tell myself that we were the boys in that newspaper article!'

'Da thinks it'll be good for business for him and for your da too.'

'Funny you should say that. People were comin' out of the woodwork yesterday looking to have their chimneys cleaned. I must say Mattie looked pretty pleased with himself when I met him this mornin'.'

'And why wouldn't he be, with all the praise he's getting for the story?' laughed Redzer.

It felt odd not sharing my new secret with my best friend,

but I had promised Mr Webb I wouldn't say a word about it – a promise I intended to keep.

Walking down Westland Row, a loud voice startled us. 'Leave us alone!'

We backtracked a few steps and peered down the nearest lane. The gate at the end was the entrance into a coachmaker's yard. In front of it, Joe Melody and four or five other boys had cornered Rats and Francis. Rats's lip was bleeding, and Francis was lying on the ground.

'Hugh!' screamed Rats. Redzer and I took one look at each other. We both thought the same thing: Joe and his gang were tough, and the two boys could end up badly hurt. Could we live with ourselves if we kept on walking?

'Stop!' I shouted, running down the alley.

'What are you talkin' about?' said Joe, rubbing the blood on his hand onto his trousers. 'Sure, weren't you the ones that –'

'You mustn't have heard the latest,' I said, trying to make my voice sound strong while I raced through ideas about what to say next.

'What are you talkin' about?' repeated Joe. Rats helped Francis to stand up. His clothes were covered with sawdust from the yard.

'These two are on their way to Daniel O'Connell's house,' I said.

'That's right,' said Rats, looking at me intently.

'They're going over to say sorry to the girl,' I added.

Rats hesitated but quickly realised this was his only way out of a further beating.

'That's what I was trying to tell you, but you kept hitting me,' he said to Joe.

'Going over to say sorry!' said Joe, almost spitting out the words. 'Bit late in the day for that, isn't it?'

'No, it's not,' said Redzer. 'I heard they're mortified about what they did. Right, Rats?'

'Right,' said Rats, elbowing Francis to agree, which he did.

'And I know Daniel O'Connell will welcome the pair of them,' I added. 'Isn't he always going on about talkin' and bein' peaceful instead of sortin' out things by fightin'?'

The mention of Daniel O'Connell had a calming effect on the boys.

'Nobody's stoppin' you,' said one of the gang. 'Off yez go.'

'We're headin' that way, too,' I said, beckoning Rats and Francis to follow. 'Are you comin'?'

Once out on the street, Rats hesitated. 'I'll have to go home and clean up first.'

'No need. You can do that in the scullery in Merrion Square,' I said.

As we walked, we got plenty of funny looks from passers-by, some because of the boys' appearance, others for the news that had spread throughout the neighbourhood about them. I never saw Rats so quiet. At Merrion Square, we went down the steps to the basement. Mrs Sullivan opened the door, and her smile disappeared when she saw the two boys with us.

'Yes?' she said to Rats.

'Mrs Sullivan, could I clean up please before we go …'

'Up to say sorry to the girl from Belfast,' continued Francis.

'In you go, the pair of you,' she said. 'You'll have to wait your turn to talk to our young lady. She's very busy this morning.'

The two boys were bundled into the scullery while we were shown to the upstairs parlour. Daniel O'Connell and Albertha were there with three reporters. Albertha wore a light-blue dress and had a lacy cap on her head covering her tufts of blond hair. She was even more like a girl than she was before.

'Ah, here are the two boys in question,' said Daniel O'Connell. 'Now I've to leave, but Mrs Sullivan will stay while you ask your questions. Boys, these men are from *The Dublin Evening Post, The Morning Register* and *The Pilot*. They're going to print their stories tomorrow.'

He spoke to Mrs Sullivan in Irish. She replied, and going by his face he must have told him that Rats and Francis were downstairs. He said something in a hurry, and off he went.

The reporters' questions were like Mattie's, with a few different ones thrown into the mix. The man from *The Pilot* was very taken with the part where Albertha met the Wren Boys and how they treated her. By this stage, everyone knew that it was Rats.

'And what about Darby Madden? Do you know if he has been found yet?' asked the *Morning Register* reporter.

'They were still lookin' for him this mornin',' said Albertha.

'Best to check with the police station about that villain,' said Mrs Sullivan from her perch in the corner. 'He can't be found soon enough or punished harshly enough as far as I'm concerned.'

They asked some more questions. When we answered, Mrs Sullivan pointed to the clock on the mantelpiece and stood up. 'That's enough for today, gentlemen. The way Albertha and the boys have answered your questions is a credit to them.'

'Just one more –'

'Good morning, gentlemen,' repeated Mrs Sullivan sternly.

'Good morning, Mrs Sullivan,' said the reporter from *The Pilot*. 'Thank you for your time.'

Once they had left, Mrs Sullivan said to come down to the kitchen, where it was warmer. 'Albertha, darlin', two boyos downstairs have come to say sorry to you. I'm sure you know who they are.'

'To say sorry?' said Albertha.

'It's up to you whether or not you want to speak to them.'

Albertha adjusted the ribbon in her hair. 'Oh, I will. I'm curious to know what they're goin' to say.'

'Go into my little parlour, and I'll bring them in,' said Mrs Sullivan. 'Hugh and Owen can wait here. I'll ask one of the girls to bring you a cup of tea and a slice of *cáca milis*.'

She ushered Albertha into the room, and seconds later, Rats and Francis passed us, looking considerably cleaner than when we saw them last. Rats, the colour of chalk, kept looking ahead, and Francis was looking down at his feet. They closed the door of the little parlour after them.

* * *

We heard voices – Albertha's was by far the loudest – but we couldn't make out the words. Twenty minutes later, Rats came out. Francis followed, his eyes red.

'Thanks,' Rats mumbled as he passed us. Francis followed and did the same.

'I'll see the pair of ye out,' said Mrs Sullivan. 'I've to pop out myself for a few minutes. She grabbed her shawl and bonnet and followed them out the door.

'That went very well,' said Albertha, stepping out of the parlour.

'It did?' I asked.

'Yes. Didn't it give me the chance to let them know what it was like for me?'

'And?'

'I found out that Francis has a sister the same age as me. "How would you feel if someone behaved to her like the pair of you did to me?" I asked him.'

'That was clever,' said Redzer. 'What did he say?'

'That if he knew I was a girl, he'd have never done it. But I soon put him right – it should never have been done to anyone, boy or girl. Sure, then he started blubberin' like a baby and couldn't say another word.'

'And what about Rats?'

'I'll have to be honest with ye, boys – I used some colourful language at first because he tried to make out that he did it as a "prank". But when he stopped and *listened* to me, I told him I couldn't understand how he could behave the way he did, comin' from such a respectable family. I know full well from listenin' to the tittle-tattle among the servants here that his father's business has been affected by what he did. That's why I brought in about the family. I asked him what his mother thought about how he behaved. His sore lip trembled, and he had to hold back the tears.'

I was impressed by Albertha's way of handling it.

'Hard to believe Rats could be like that,' said Redzer.

'Did they tell you why they came here in the first place?' I asked.

'They did,' said Albertha. 'And I said the very least they could do was to thank you on the way out for saving them.'

'It'll be strange meeting them again. I wonder how they'll be with us?' I said.

'I'd say Rats'll be cautious about what he says and will have as little to do with us as possible,' said Redzer. 'And that's perfectly fine with me.'

'Any news from home?' I asked Albertha.

'Mr O'Connell's written to my aunt and to the minister.

He hopes to hear back from them early next week.' She lowered her voice. 'He's been so kind to me, and I feel terrible now for callin' him the Bully Beggarman. You'll never tell anyone that, I hope? I made Rats and Francis promise they wouldn't.'

We both assured her we wouldn't.

'How are you getting on with Mrs Sullivan?' asked Redzer.

'Very well. A kind wee woman, surely, though sometimes I don't understand a word comin' out of her mouth, and I know she has trouble understandin' me. You know what's strange, though ... Nobody saw me when I was workin' as a climbing boy. I may as well have been invisible. Now that I'm in the lap of luxury in Mr O'Connell's house and the story's in the paper, people are falling over themselves to help me.'

I knew what she meant about being invisible when covered in coaldust. I often felt that way too and wondered had I imagined it.

'Yes, and presents comin' in,' she continued. 'Some local bookseller found out I like *Robinson Crusoe* and sent me a copy to keep. And a dressmaker called this mornin' and measured me for a new wee dress.'

I smiled as I thought of the little group in Mr O'Neill's. So they really were serious when they said they'd help.

'And the best one of all: the Italian singing teacher Izzy works for arrived just before the pair of ye. Said he wants to give a concert to raise money for me!'

Chapter Twenty-One

Two Weeks Later

I was given the task of reading an article for the family and neighbours who had gathered in our kitchen one morning.

UPDATE ON THE ALBERTHA MCCOY STORY

Thanks to help from the public, the search for chimney sweep Darby Madden ended yesterday when constables in Naas, County Kildare, found him hiding in an outhouse on a farm on the Blessington Road. He is currently in Kilmainham Gaol, awaiting trial.

The editor of this newspaper has received several letters inquiring about Albertha McCoy and whether contact has been made with her mother or aunt. Mr Daniel O'Connell received a letter from the Rev George Nicholson, Belfast, to say that Albertha's mother is in hospital but is recovering well. Thanks to the money raised by Signor Antonio Sapio's concert and to private donations, both mother and daughter will move to a new address as soon as she is discharged. We also contacted Mrs Sutton, Albertha's aunt.

'I'm relieved to learn my niece is safe and well,' she said. 'A sincere thanks to everyone who has helped her.'

We are happy to provide an update on the three gallant children who saved Miss McCoy. Firstly, Hugh O'Dare has been offered a position as an apprentice clerk with the printer Mr Richard Webb in South William Street.

'He has a tremendous head for figures,' said his former teacher, Brother Maloney. 'Both teachers and pupils in the Boys' School in Hanover Street wish him every success.'

'Wait,' said Uncle Phonsie. 'They never said you were bein' provided with room and board.'

'They don't put that sort of thing into the newspapers,' I said, but the pride in my uncle's voice was unmistakable. Starting a job and moving to a house where I was to have my own bedroom would surely be a new experience. I continued reading.

Secondly, thanks to the reception Miss Izzy Everard received when she sang 'The Last Rose of Summer' at Mr Sapio's concert, she is to receive lessons from the singing master.

'I heard that girl could make a livin' at the singin' yet,' said Ma. 'Scholar here was at the concert and –'

I could feel my face heat up, so I continued reading the article before anyone noticed.

Thirdly, due to the expansion of the family business, Owen Lampkin has started work with his father as an apprentice carpenter.

'It doesn't say anythin' about the Lampkins gettin' the contract for buildin' the new church,' said Ma when I paused to take a breath.

'It hasn't gone public yet,' said Da.

'There's more – let me finish,' I said.

Harmony Yard, the Manure and Soot Yard owned by the Lampkin family, will now be managed by Mr Bartle O'Dare, Hugh O'Dare's father.

'*Managed*, no less,' said Uncle Phonsie. 'We're mixin' with very grand people now.'

Ma laughed. 'Wasn't it lucky that the Lampkins didn't sell the yard?'

'It was,' Da said. 'It looks like Charlie Rattigan's business isn't on the rise as he thought it'd be. The way his young lad behaved has people avoidin' him, I believe.'

'Even though Scholar said he went to the girl to say sorry,' said Ma.

'Did they say anything about me in the paper?' asked Tim. 'About Harmony Yard? Don't forget, I'm to be the assistant manager.'

Everyone laughed at this. Tim was to give a hand to Da after school.

'How are you goin' to manage with your arm, Bartle?' asked Fred Callan.

'Other than Tim, one of Tom Lampkin's workers is helpin'' out 'til it mends.'

'There's more. Are you listening, everyone?' I said.

The Society for Superseding the Necessity of Climbing Boys has shared this story far and wide to illustrate the misery and cruelty associated with children cleaning chimneys. They insist that the law should be changed and that it should be illegal for boys and girls under the age of fourteen to be employed in this work. We have also been informed that the society has been in contact with the O'Dare family. They will be presenting them with a machine for cleaning chimneys on Monday. Bartle O'Dare said that his two sons will continue with the business and are looking forward to using the machine. They are also happy to report that they are fully booked until the first of February.

Everyone started clapping.

'Tom Lampkin said we can keep the machine in the hut in Harmony Yard,' said Dexie.

'Signor Sapio said he'd be over on Monday for the presentation,' I told them. 'Also, Izzy will be comin' too.'

Dexie winked at me. 'We'll look forward to that.'

No more pretending. No more hiding the truth. I felt proud of my family. I felt proud of myself! I folded the newspaper and sat on one of the crates. A new year, a new start. I thought returning to school would be the only way forward for me. Little did I know I'd be offered a job as a clerk, let alone one that came with room and board. Brother Maloney told me he'd be teaching night classes in navigation if I still wanted to learn about it, so I put my name down. The future seemed to stretch forward like one of Sinbad's adventures. I was 'all aboard' and excited to discover what would happen next.

Historical Themes

Climbing Boys

When I tell people I have written a story about climbing boys set in Dublin, I am often met with, 'I thought they only worked in cities and towns in England'. But Irish cities and towns grew in the eighteenth and nineteenth centuries, and many houses had two storeys or more. Coal was increasingly used in these houses – a fuel that needed a good draught to keep burning. This meant fireplaces needed to be smaller and chimney flues narrower. As a result, chimneys needed to be 'swept' or cleaned more frequently. Sadly, the solution for cleaning these narrow chimney flues was the same as in England: to employ young boys and occasionally girls, usually from the poorest families.

Readers may think that the kidnapping of Albertha in my story was purely the stuff of fiction, but in real life, some children were kidnapped to work as climbing boys. In a small number of extreme situations, very poor parents sold their children to chimney sweeps.

The death of climbing boy Bob O'Leary, referred to by Daniel O'Connell and others in the book, also reflects the horrific accounts of such deaths recorded in the newspapers. For climbing boys who survived, injuries and illnesses ranged from cuts, scars and burns to stooped backs and cancer.

From the end of the eighteenth century and throughout the nineteenth century, groups of people campaigned to stop the use of climbing boys and promote the use of cleaning machines instead. *The Water-Babies* by Charles Kingsley, a famous book published in 1863, aroused widespread sympathy for climbing boys. Although various Acts of Parliament were passed, it wasn't until 1875 that climbing boys were no longer allowed to be employed.

Ireland in 1830

Daniel O'Connell was a major figure in Ireland. He won an election in Co Clare in 1828 but could not take his seat in parliament because he was Catholic, even though he and the Catholic Association had been campaigning for years to change the law. In 1829, they were successful. The Catholic Emancipation Bill was passed, allowing Catholics to become members of parliament, and O'Connell became known as 'The Liberator'. As he had a house in Merrion Square, I thought it would be an excellent way to involve him in the story by having Scholar clean his chimney!

Valuable information about Dublin in those days can be

found in directories such as the *Dublin Almanac and General Register of Ireland* (1835). Among the names listed were Signor Sapio, 'professor of singing', and Richard D. Webb, 'printer'. The *Almanac* also includes addresses of various shops and businesses. This helped me imagine what my characters might see, hear, or even smell as they walked the streets of Dublin.

A major inquiry into education was going on in Ireland in the 1820s. From time to time, the 'commissioners' published reports on their findings. I was fascinated to find out that among the subjects taught in the Christian Brothers' school in Hanover Street were book-keeping, navigation, algebra and geometry. During the same time, the government was investigating the lives of poor people. The findings armed me with helpful details about the poor of Dublin.

As always, I found the newspapers one of the best sources to draw from. I saw an advertisement for the pantomime *Robinson Crusoe* in *The Evening Packet*, to take place in the New Adelphi Theatre, Great Brunswick Street. I wanted to include it, but I knew Scholar couldn't afford an entrance ticket, so I used it in his chase of 'Bert' on St Stephen's night. To find out about Saint Andrew's Church, I scanned the papers for articles about the churches built in Dublin in 1830 to learn how money was being collected to pay for them.

Advertisements for houses and businesses provided details about places where our characters lived and worked, what pastimes they might have had, and what they might have eaten and drunk. Reports of the major events happening at the time were also valuable, such as the address of the tradesmen to Daniel O'Connell in December 1830.

Ann Murtagh, 2023

Also from The O'Brien Press

The Sound of Freedom
Ann Murtagh

It's spring 1919, and Ireland's War of Independence has broken out. In a cottage in County Westmeath, thirteen-year-old Colm Conneely longs to join the local Volunteers, the 'Rainbow Chasers' who are fighting for an Ireland free from English rule. But Colm has another ambition too – to make a new life in America, working as a fiddle player and involved in the republican movement there.

When spirited Belfast girl Alice McCluskey – who speaks Irish, shares his love of Irish music and is also committed to 'the cause' – arrives in town, Colm's dreams take a new turn. Where will his talent lead him? And how will a long-held family secret shape his future?

'Action-packed … I just couldn't put it down.'
– *Ireland's Own*

'[A] well-crafted tale not only bringing Irish history to a new generation but entwining readers young and not-so young in a web of intrigue and family secrets.' – *Evening Echo*

The Kidds of Summerhill
Ann Murtagh

It is spring 1945, and orphaned Nancy Kidd has a lot on her plate as head of the family. The 'Cruelty Men' could send her and her siblings to the dreaded industrial schools. One of their spies lives in the same tenement building and holds a grudge against the Kidds.

More trouble is the last thing Nancy needs, but that's just what she gets when she tries to help a friend in need. Just as her life begins to unravel, she meets Karla, a Jewish refugee from Prague who might know a way out.

'Nancy's first-person narration is a pleasure to read. Murtagh is fast becoming one of our most accomplished historical novelists for children.'
— *Irish Independent*

'Filled with accurate historical detail, telling a story of family struggle, it is full of life, hope, steadfastness and with moments of humour and delight. A simply marvellous story.' — *Fallen Star Stories*

Growing up with

tots to teens and in between

Why CHILDREN love O'Brien:

Over 350 books for all ages, including
picture books, humour, fiction, true stories,
nature and more

Why TEACHERS love O'Brien:

Hundreds of activities and teaching guides,
created by teachers for teachers,
all FREE to download from obrien.ie

Visit, explore, buy
obrien.ie